Colliding Into Your Love

KYIRIS ASHLEY

U.A.D PRESENTS

Stay Up to Date

To stay up to date on new releases, plus get information on contests, sneak peeks and more,

Click the link below...
https://mailchi.mp/6d21003686d1/subscribe

Soundtracks

Scan the QR Code below to listen to the Soundtracks/Singles of some of your favorite U.A.D titles:

Don't have Spotify or Apple Music?
No Sweat!
Visit your choice streaming platform and search URBAN AINT DEAD.

Currently on lock serving a bid?
JPay, iHeartRadio, WHATEVER!

We got you covered.
Simply log into your facility's kiosk or tablet, go to music and
search URBAN AINT DEAD.

URBAN AINT DEAD PRESENTS

Like & Follow us on social media:

FB - URBAN AINT DEAD

IG: @uadpresents

Tik Tok - @uadpresents

Submission Guidelines

Submit the first three chapters of your completed manuscript to urbanaintdead@gmail.com, subject line: Your book's title. The manuscript must be in a .doc file and sent as an attachment. The document should be in Times New Roman, double-spaced, and in size 12 font. Also, provide your synopsis and full contact information. If sending multiple submissions, they must each be in a separate email. Have a story but no way to submit it electronically? You can still submit to URBAN AINT DEAD. Send in the first three chapters, written or typed, of your completed manuscript to:

URBAN AINT DEAD
P.O Box 448
Maybrook, NY 12543

DO NOT send original manuscript. Must be a duplicate.
Provide your synopsis and a cover letter containing your full contact information.
Thanks for considering URBAN AINT DEAD.

Note From The Author

Hey, y'all. What up doe, my baby? I'm just a girl from the east side of Detroit with a dream and a pen. I'll never forget when I started writing my first book. It was November 1, 2019. I'd been writing all my life, but that was the first time I had actually considered myself an author. I didn't know much about self-publishing, but I told myself I was going to learn everything I needed to so that I could publish my book myself. I found a great editor and got that shit rollin'.

I'd planned on releasing the book the following year on my late grandmother's birthday, which was May 9th, 2020; however, Amazon had other plans. My book wasn't released until May 16th. After that, I continued to write and self-publish. I didn't have a lot of readers, but I continued to write because I knew it was my passion.

Then, in 2021, I met Elijah R. Freeman, who told me about his publishing company, Urban Ain't Dead. I wouldn't be me if I wasn't real with y'all, so I will say the first time we talked about it, I told him no, not because I didn't believe in him but because I wanted to do shit my way. But that didn't matter. Elijah still showed up, still supported me and my work, putting me in my first magazine later that same year. I continued to self-publish my books. But as the saying goes, if it's meant to be, then it will be.

Because what God has for you is for you. Needless to say, I signed to UAD in 2022, and this feels like home. I got so much love for you, E, and I'm proud to call you my brother.

To my sistas, Nai, Paris Iman, and Keely, I love y'all down! Y'all keep me grounded when shit gets rough. I came in this game with just me and now have a family that's ten toes behind me just like I am with them. I can't wait to scream, "We did it!" I could say so much more about y'all, but what's understood don't have to be explained.

To my editor, Shawna Brim, I know I be puttin' you through it lol, but you always get it done. We could be down to the wire, working off no sleep, but we be locked in together. I love your soul, baby cakes. Thank you for being the other parent to so many of my book babies lol.

To my loyal readers, if you been down since *Blended Families,* then we basically locked in or whatevea Cardi B say. Y'all really fuck wit' the kid, and that is so amazing to me. Thank you for all of your continuous support. This is book number 20, and I'm just getting started!

To all of my new readers, heyyy, y'all. I'm Kyiris (pronounced Key-iris), aka The Key To Urban Fiction. I hope y'all ready because y'all gonna be seeing a lot more of me.

And last but definitely not least.... To my pen, thank you to my pen!

I hope y'all enjoy the book!

Chapter One

Brielle sat on the toilet, watching as the two pink lines appeared on the pregnancy test she was holding in her hand. Her heart dropped in disbelief, as her eyes darted to the box the test came in. The two pink lines meant she was pregnant, and a small smile spread across her face. She couldn't believe she was pregnant with her first child. Brielle had never been pregnant before, and the joy that filled her was unmatched. After wiping herself, she washed her hands and went directly to her closet to pick out something to wear. She wanted to look good when she told her boyfriend the news. Although they hadn't been trying to get pregnant, they hadn't done anything to prevent it either.

Brielle chose a black one-piece that snatched her waist and hugged her curves. She laid it across the gray chaise that sat in the corner of her room before heading to the shower. Brielle was all smiles, as she washed her body, thinking of the way Delano would react when she told him she was going to have his child. In that short moment, Brielle pictured their entire lives together. Her giving birth with Delano by her side. Them getting married, having more children, and living a beautiful life together. She couldn't wait to live out her dreams with the man she was in love with.

Brielle walked back into her bedroom and rubbed lotion into

her skin before getting dressed. She stood in front of her mirror, turning slightly from side to side, as she checked her reflection. The black one-piece clung to her body, accentuating every curve she carried with ease. At five feet one, she wasn't tall, but her frame was thick in all the right places. She had hips that demanded attention and thick thighs that led to a round backside.

She tugged on a black cropped bubble jacket, zipping it halfway up. The jacket added bulk, but it didn't take away from the way the one-piece hugged her body underneath. Her skin was a light golden-brown and glowed under the warm bedroom light. Her long, blonde box braids were freshly done, and her baby hairs were already laid to perfection.

Bending down, Brielle laced up her wheat colored Timbs, adding just a little color to her all-black outfit. When she stood again, she searched the small tray of perfumes on her dresser, looking for a fragrance to wear. Instead of picking from one of the two new perfumes she had, she reached for one of her favorites, Ari by Ariana Grande. She spritzed once on both sides of her neck and twice on the back. She also spritzed both wrists before adding several sprays to her clothes.

Leaning toward the mirror, she applied clear gloss to her lips before rubbing them together. Her long lash extensions were placed along her almond shaped eyes perfectly, so she knew all she needed was a touch of gloss. After she placed her gold hoops in her ears and grabbed her black Steve Madden bag, she was ready to go.

She walked outside, and the cool October air hit her. It was four in the afternoon, and with the season changing, it seemed later than it actually was. Brielle hopped into her Honda Civic, allowing the older model car to warm up a bit before she pulled off. She then took the fifteen-minute drive to Delano's loft in downtown Detroit.

Brielle had been with Delano for an entire year, and she really loved him. They met one night at a club her best friend, Amya, had all but dragged her to one Saturday night, and the two had been inseparable ever since. Delano stood six feet even with a slim frame and small muscles. He had dark skin that was as smooth as chocolate and locs that hung to his shoulders. He was everything that Brielle wanted in a man – fine, hardworking, loving, and a provider. To Brielle, he was the perfect man, always being there for her anytime she needed him. She walked up to his door, knocking on it softly, before it opened.

"Hey, baby. I didn't know we had plans for tonight. Did I forget something?" Delano asked, bringing Brielle in for a hug. He kissed her lips softly before she answered.

"No, you didn't forget anything. We didn't have plans for tonight. I just wanted to see you, maybe share some good news."

"Oh, yeah? Come sit down and tell yo' man this good news you got."

Delano led Brielle to the couch, and they both sat down. He turned to her, letting her know that she had his full attention.

Brielle smiled, grabbing his hand. "Baby, I'm pregnant. You're going to be a daddy."

She watched as the smile Delano had turned into a cold stare. "Stop playin' so much. What's the good news?" he asked.

Brielle let go of his hand and reached for her purse, pulling out the pregnancy test, showing him the two pink lines in the small box on the front of the test.

"I'm serious, baby. We are about to bring a child into this world. We gonna be parents."

"No the fuck we not." Delano recoiled. "If you pregnant, you gon' have to handle that and quickly."

"Handle it? What does that mean, Delano? This baby is a blessing. It's a symbol of our love. So, tell me what does handle it mean?"

"It means take care of that shit. I don't want no kids, and you knew that shit from jump. Now, you comin' over here, smiling, tellin' me you pregnant? Fuck is you on, Bri?"

"Did you know you didn't want kids when you was fucking me raw?"

"Bitch, I pulled out. You think you 'bout to trap me with a fuckin' baby that you already know I don't want? Fuck is wrong with you? See, this the problem with y'all bitches now. A nigga tell y'all that he don't want no fuckin' kids, and y'all think y'all can change the nigga. Then get mad when y'all become single mamas. Save yourself the trouble of being a single mama, Brielle, and get a damn abortion. I'll even pay for it."

Brielle was stunned, as she sat there with her mouth wide open. She couldn't believe the things that were coming out of Delano's mouth. This was the same man that told her that he loved her and couldn't picture his life without her just yesterday. Now, here he was, telling her to abort their child because he didn't want it. Tears began to form in her eyes, as she looked at him, hoping that this was some type of cruel joke.

"Delano, you can't be serious. You want me to have an abortion? Why? This is what people that are in love do. They have children, get married, and build a life together. Why are you trying to tear it all down? This could be beautiful. Why do you want to ruin it?"

"My life is already beautiful, and I got everything I want. Kids, especially by you, was never something I saw or wanted in my future. We havin' fun. Why the fuck would you want to ruin that with a baby?"

Brielle stood to her feet with those words. "What the fuck you mean, especially by me? Are we not happy? Because I thought we were."

"Yes, we were until you brought yo' ass in here tellin' me this bullshit. This was supposed to be fun. Now, you over here tryna trap me with a baby that you know I don't fuckin' want."

"Trap you?! Delano, I didn't fuck myself and get pregnant. And who the fuck are you to trap? I can't believe you even saying this shit to me. You know what, Delano? Fuck you!"

Brielle grabbed her purse and stormed out of Delano's loft, her chest tight, eyes burning with unshed tears. The slam of the door echoed behind her, but it couldn't drown out the words that kept replaying in her head – Delano telling her that he didn't want the baby. Her steps were quick and uneven, almost frantic, as she made her way down the hall. The whole ride over, she had imagined this moment going differently. She had pictured his face lighting up, his arms wrapping around her, his voice promising her they'd be a family. She thought this was the beginning of something solid, something real. Instead, his rejection hit harder than any punch his fist could have thrown.

Her mind raced, as she hit the stairwell, clutching the railing like it might hold her together. She couldn't understand it. They had been together for a year – a whole year of late-night talks, weekends spent wrapped up in each other, and whispers about the future. How could he turn around and act like none of that mattered? By the time she reached the front door, a tear had finally escaped, sliding down her cheek. She brushed it away roughly, angry at herself for even crying over him. But the truth hurt. She thought they were building something. She thought he loved her enough to want this next step.

Instead, he had looked her dead in the eye and told her no – no to her, no to the baby she was carrying, and no to the family she thought they were about to create together. Brielle pulled her bubble coat tighter around herself, as she pushed through the door and into the cold air. The wind hit her face, stinging, but it was nothing compared to the ache in her chest. Brielle cried the entire drive home. When she got there, she went directly to her room, took off her clothes, and crawled into bed. She stayed there for the rest of the night, crying until she finally drifted off to sleep.

Chapter Two

Two weeks had passed since Brielle had walked out of Delano's loft with her heart cracked wide open. In all that time, not a single text or call had come through from his number. The silence between them felt heavier than the words he'd thrown at her, but it was also clarifying. If he didn't want her baby, fine. She wasn't going to beg him to be part of their lives. The decision had settled in her bones like stone. She was keeping her baby. Whether Delano was going to stand beside her or not, she wasn't about to let anybody make her feel like her child wasn't worth having.

One Friday night, she sat in her small living room, which was dimly lit by the flicker of the TV. A half-empty bowl of popcorn sat on the glass coffee table in front of her, the buttery smell still lingering in the air. A fleece blanket was pulled across her lap, her legs tucked up underneath her, as she sat curled into the corner of the couch. *About Last Night* played on the screen, but her attention wasn't really on it. Every few minutes, she found herself glancing down at her stomach, hand brushing over the slight swell that only she seemed to notice.

Her braids were tied up in a loose bun, and she wore an oversized white T-shirt and a pair of black leggings. Just as she reached for another handful of popcorn, her phone lit up on the couch cushion beside her. The vibration buzzed against her leg, startling her. She glanced at the phone and froze when she saw Delano's picture flashing on her screen. Her heart stuttered then raced, thudding hard against her chest. For two weeks, he had been silent, and now, out of nowhere, he was calling. Questions flooded her mind all at once. *What can he possibly want? Why now? Does he regret what he said? Does he even care?*

Her hand hovered over the phone for a moment, hesitation locking her in place. Part of her wanted to send it to voicemail, let him sit in the silence the way she had been forced to. But another part of her ached to hear his voice again. With a shaky breath, Brielle pressed accept and slowly lifted the phone to her ear.

"Hello?" she whispered, her voice barely steady.

"Bri, why haven't I heard from you? It's been weeks, and you haven't called at all."

Brielle paused, removing the phone from her ear and looking down at it, making sure she'd heard him right. The last time she spoke with him, he was telling her to get rid of their child. Now, here he was, asking her why he hadn't heard from her. Before she could answer, Delano continued to speak.

"I don't think our last conversation ended well, and that's not what I want. How 'bout you come over tomorrow for brunch? We can sit and eat and have a real conversation. Things got way too heated last time, and that's not us."

"Yeah, I agree. Things went all the way left. So, yeah, I'll come over tomorrow, and we can have a real conversation."

"Okay, I'll see you tomorrow. Let's say eleven, and we can talk."

Brielle agreed before ending the call. For a moment, she just sat there, replaying their conversation in her head. She was happy that he wanted to talk, and she hoped he would apologize for the fucked-up things he'd said when she first told him she was pregnant. Brielle loved Delano, and all she wanted was for them to be a family. She sat there on her couch, now feeling a hundred times better than she did before Delano's call. She watched a few more movies before she finally went to her bedroom and went to sleep.

Brielle had set her alarm for eight that next morning, wanting to get up early so that she could take her time getting dressed. She wanted to look her best when she saw Delano. She wanted him to see that no other woman would be able to carry his child the way she could – still looking good.

Getting out of bed, she went directly to the bathroom to shower and brush her teeth. Once she was done, she went into her closet to find something to wear. After about fifteen minutes, she'd finally settled on a chocolate brown turtleneck with matching chocolate brown leather pants. She styled her braids in a half up half down style before placing edge control on her baby hairs and swooping them to perfection.

Brielle slid into her clothes before slipping her feet into leather knee high boots that were the same color brown as the rest of her outfit. She placed a pair of gold hoops into her ears before placing gold jewelry around her neck and wrist. She sprayed herself with YSL Libre, a birthday gift from Delano that he loved smelling on her. Once Brielle glossed her full lips, she was ready to go.

The drive over to Delano's loft was filled with anticipation for the conversation they would have. *He didn't mean none of that shit he said to me. He was just scared and didn't know what to do. That's why he wants to make up for it today, and I'm going to let him,* she thought. She parked her car and made her way up to Delano's loft. She knocked on the door, and he answered seconds after with a smile on his face.

"Hey, baby, I missed you," Delano greeted, bringing Brielle in for a hug. "Don't go that long without takin' to me again."

"I didn't know where we stood after our last conversation. Things got pretty heated."

"Don't even worry about that right now. I know we both said some shit that we didn't mean. We can handle all that later. Right now, I want us to enjoy this meal and each other."

Brielle nodded her head, agreeing with Delano. She set her purse down on the coffee table and took off her jacket, laying it neatly across the black leather sofa. Delano took her hand and led her to the small dining room table. He pulled out her chair before motioning for Brielle to take her seat. He walked into the kitchen and grabbed the two plates he'd placed in the oven before walking back over to Brielle. She watched as he placed a plate of steak, potatoes, eggs, and biscuits in front of her.

"This looks delicious. Thank you." Brielle smiled.

"Only the best for you, baby."

The moment the words left his lips, Brielle lost her appetite. She picked at her plate, her fork scraping against the edge, as she tried to force herself to eat. Her stomach wasn't queasy – not exactly. It was her nerves, the uncertainty of why he had even called her after two weeks of silence only to not want to talk about her pregnancy. He sat across from her, looking as unbothered as ever, like he didn't have a care in the world. When he spoke, it was about everything yet nothing at all. He told her about the new client he picked up at work. About the shoes he had on preorder and couldn't wait to come. About trips he wanted to take, but nothing about the one thing that mattered.

Brielle nodded along, forcing small smiles when he looked her way. But inside, her thoughts screamed. She wanted to slam her hands on the table and make him say the words, make him acknowledge the life growing inside of her. Yet she stayed quiet, swallowing back the questions burning in her chest. She didn't want to scare him away. If he had to ease into being a father, she would let him, as long as he was ready by the time she gave birth. When the food was gone and their plates were pushed aside, Delano leaned back in his chair, studying her with those dark eyes that, up until now, had never been hard to read.

"C'mon," he said finally, standing up and holding out a hand.

Brielle hesitated but slid her fingers into his. His grip was warm and steady, and before she could ask what he was doing, he pulled her to her feet. Without another word, he led her down the short hall toward his bedroom, swinging the door open, so they could walk inside. Delano pulled Brielle close to him, kissing her passionately.

"Delano, wait." Brielle placed her hand on his chest, pushing him back just a little. "We need to talk before we go any further."

"We can talk later. Right now, I want to taste you."

Without another word, Delano began pulling off Brielle's clothes. She tried to stop him, halfheartedly, but the truth was that Brielle was weak for him. She wanted him just as badly as he wanted her. So, when Delano lifted her and laid her on his bed, she opened her legs for him and allowed him to nestle his head between her thighs. She moaned the moment his tongue flickered over her clit, grabbing his head and pushing him deeper. His licks were soft and wet, and when he reached up to play with her nipples as he licked, Brielle lost it.

"Yesssss, Delano. Just like that," she moaned.

Delano kept going, knowing this was exactly what she needed. When Brielle wrapped her legs around his shoulders, he moved them, placing them in the air, before sliding his tongue down from her clit to her crack.

"Fuckkkkk!" Brielle breathed before biting her bottom lip.

When Brielle's legs began shaking uncontrollably, he let them down slowly before climbing on top of her. She opened for him immediately, wrapping her legs around his waist as she took him in. His manhood filled her, and he groaned, as her tightness wrapped around him. Delano planted kisses on her neck and chest with each pump into her wetness.

"You feel so good, baby. Tell me whose pussy this is," Delano ordered.

"It's yours, Daddy. This pussy belongs to you."

With those words, Delano went deeper, spilling his seed into her already pregnant womb. Delano kissed Brielle one last time before rolling off of her and walking into his bathroom. He came back a few moments later with a warm towel for Brielle. Delano laid back onto the bed, grabbing the remote and turning on the TV. He pulled Brielle close to him, holding her tightly, as he picked something for them to watch.

Around seven that evening, they had watched two movies and fucked two more times. Delano reached over to his nightstand and grabbed his phone.

"You hungry?" he asked, opening the Door Dash app on his phone.

"Starving. What you got a taste for?"

"I want Chinese, but you know I only eat Golden Bowl, so if that shit ain't on Door Dash, then I'ma have to think of something else."

"Yeah, that shit sounds good. If it's on there, I want some egg fu yong and some sweet and sour shrimp. And you know I gotta have the shrimp fried rice and white rice."

"I got you, and that shit on here. We 'bout to eat good."

Delano placed the order, and Brielle went to take a shower, while they waited on the food. After the hot shower, she wrapped herself in one of Delano's plush towels and walked back into his bedroom. Delano wasn't laying in bed anymore, and she hoped he was at the door getting the food. She made her way to his drawer and pulled out one of his white t-shirts before putting it on. Brielle crawled up into bed and picked another movie, as she waited on Delano to return.

He walked back into the room, holding the bag of takeout, paper plates, cups, and a Pepsi. Brielle smiled, sitting up in bed and positioning two pillows behind her back, so she could get comfortable.

"What's this you got us watching now?" Delano asked, getting in the bed before handing Brielle a plate.

"*Welcome Home Roscoe Jenkins*. I loved this movie."

Delano rolled his eyes, as he opened the bag of food and pulled out the items. "We can watch this, but I'm pickin' the next movie."

They ate and watched movies for the rest of the night before they both ended up falling asleep.

Chapter Three

Brielle woke up the next morning, still laying next to Delano. She sat up, looking over at the clock that sat on his nightstand to see it was just after nine. She was just about to get out of bed when Delano wrapped his arm around her.

"Where you going?" he asked, voice still thick with sleep.

"To the bathroom."

Delano sat up and looked over at the clock. "You want to go to breakfast or something?"

Brielle sighed, shaking her head no, before walking to the bathroom. She only had one thing on her mind that morning, and it was the baby that she was carrying. She'd allowed him not to talk about it the night before, but now, it was time to have a real talk. So, after she used the bathroom and washed her hands, she headed back to Delano's room. She took a seat on his bed, turning to speak, but before she could, Delano handed her a wad of money.

Brielle looked up at him, perplexed. "What's this?"

"That's for you. It's five grand. You can take care of a few things with that. Most importantly, you can take care of that little situation you got. With the rest, you can get you something nice, maybe some new clothes for the trip I'm going to take you on.

What's the going price for abortions nowadays, 'bout five, six hundred?"

Brielle didn't know what to say, as she looked up at him. *Is this nigga really handing me money for a fuckin' abortion? Man, what the fuck is wrong with him?*

"Delano, I'm not havin' an abortion. I can't even believe you would suggest something like that. This is our child that is growing inside of me, and you just want me to kill it? This is our chance to have a family and live the dream."

"Whose fuckin' dream is that 'cause it's sure as hell ain't mine. I told you, Brielle. I don't want no fuckin' kids with you, and that ain't changed. Now, what you can do is get rid of that thing, and we can continue to have a good time like we been doing, or you can go against me and have that baby. But if you do, I ain't gon' have nothing to do with you or that fuckin' kid. I told you already. You not gon' trap me."

"Trap you? Nigga, please stop saying that shit. I didn't beg or force you to fuck me raw. And I damn sure ain't gon' beg you to be a father to our child. My mama raised me by herself, so I can do the same if need be. Fuck you and that money. I don't fuckin' need you."

Brielle gathered her clothes and put them on before grabbing her purse and storming out of Delano's loft. She wasn't surprised at all when he didn't even try to stop her. She got into her car, peeling out the parking lot, as she headed home with tears in her eyes. She couldn't believe that she had been stupid enough to give her body to him again after the way he reacted when she first told him that she was pregnant.

Her phone rang, and she didn't even bother retrieving it from her purse. She didn't care who was calling. Her heart was broken into a million pieces, and she didn't know how she was going to get through it. She thought she would be with Delano forever, and now, all her dreams were washed away with tears.

When Brielle arrived home, she went right to her room, took her clothes off, and got into her bed. Tears fell from her eyes, as she thought of what had gotten them to this point. *When did Delano stop loving me? Or did he not love me to begin with?*

Brielle stayed in bed all day, ignoring calls and text messages. She didn't want to talk to anyone; all she wanted to do was cry. And that was all she did for the rest of the day and well into the night.

When Brielle finally got out of bed, it was seven o'clock the next morning. Her stomach was empty, and her bladder was full. She walked into the bathroom, relieving herself, before washing her hands, her face, and brushing her teeth. When she was done, she went to the kitchen to make herself some breakfast. She cooked sausage, eggs, and toast, poured herself a glass of apple juice, and took a seat at her kitchen table. She still hadn't checked her phone since she left Delano's house the day before and knew it had to be dead. So, when she finished eating, she put it on the charger before taking a shower.

She'd done enough crying the night before and decided it was time to get herself together. She refused to stay depressed because of what the next muthafucka didn't want to do. Wanting to use retail therapy as an outlet, she decided to go to the mall. Brielle dressed in a pair of black joggers with a matching jacket. She slid her feet into a pair of black and white panda Dunks before spraying herself with Carolina Herrera's Good Girl. Grabbing her purse and her phone from the charger, she made her way to her car.

Summer Walker played through her car speakers as she drove. Brielle let the music fill the silence, as she cruised up I-75, one hand resting on her stomach. The baby wasn't showing yet, but she already felt protective, like every decision she made now had a purpose. Somerset came into view, gleaming in the late-morning sun. Pulling into the parking lot, she felt a twinge of excitement. Something about walking into that mall always lifted her mood. She parked, slipped on her shades, and got out the car.

The first store she wandered into was Zara. Racks of new-season clothes surrounded her, and she smiled. She ran her fingers over a camel trench coat, feeling the soft fabric.

"Oh, this is nice," she spoke out loud to herself.

She tried it on, cinched the belt around her waist, and admired the way it hugged her frame. At five-one, some coats swallowed her whole, but this one hit just right. The price tag on the coat was a hundred and forty-nine dollars, which made her hesitate for a moment, but she shrugged. *I deserve it.* Picking the coat up, she walked around the store, gathering other items that caught her eye. Brielle left Zara with two shopping bags swinging at her side.

Her next stop was Steve Madden. Shoes had always been her weakness. Rows of heels glittered beneath bright lights, and she smiled, as she looked around the store.

"Can I help you find something?" the sales associate asked, smiling.

"I'm just looking right now," Brielle replied easily, scanning the display. She spotted a pair of crisp white platform sneakers with gold accents and felt her spirits lift a little. They were casual but fly, and she knew she needed them in her closet.

When she slipped them on, she grinned. "Yeah," she said softly, "these are coming home with me."

By the time she hit Sephora, her energy had shifted. She wasn't walking around heavy anymore; her steps were lighter, as she walked through the store with her head held high. The smell hit her the moment she stepped inside – sweet florals, warm vanilla, a faint trace of something musky. For Brielle, it was Heaven. She made a beeline for the perfume section, weaving past displays of Fenty Skin and Too Faced palettes until she reached the glass shelves lined with bottles that shimmered under the spotlights. Brielle didn't want something light or girly today. She wanted something bold and sexy.

A tall associate with long, red nails approached. "Looking for a new scent today?"

"Yeah," Brielle replied, smiling faintly. "Something sexy, grown woman sexy, and not too sweet."

The associate nodded knowingly and reached for a sleek,

black bottle. "Try this. It's Black Orchid by Tom Ford. Definitely a statement fragrance."

Brielle sprayed it on a test strip, lifted it to her nose, and closed her eyes. The scent hit immediately – rich and dark with hints of jasmine and patchouli. It was bold yet still elegant.

"Mmm," she exhaled. "That's it. That's the one."

She didn't even ask the price until she was at the register – two hundred dollars plus tax. Normally, she'd flinch, but today, she handed over her card without hesitation. Smelling good had always been her armor, and she needed to feel powerful again. When the cashier placed the black Tom Ford bag into her hands, Brielle smiled.

Across from Sephora sat MAC Cosmetics, and since she was already in self-care mode, she walked right in. She sampled a few lip colors, finally choosing a nude gloss with a touch of shimmer. It looked perfect against her skin tone – subtle but sexy.

"Anything else today?" the cashier asked.

Brielle thought for a second then added a concealer and a setting spray to her basket. "Might as well," she said with a shrug. "New chapter, new face."

By the time she left the second level of the mall, she had several bags looped over her arm, along with a smoothie from the food court that she sipped as she walked. She found herself pausing in front of the Apple store, looking at the new iPhone display. Delano had promised to buy her the new model a few weeks ago, although she knew she wasn't getting it from him anymore. She considered it for a second then shook her head. *I'll get it myself later.*

Her final stop was Bath & Body Works, wanting to stock up on some new candles. She walked in, smelling a few, before picking out three. Mahogany Teakwood, Champagne Toast, and Eucalyptus Rain. She imagined her bathroom glowing with candles and filled with soft music, as she soaked in a tub full of bubbles.

When she stepped back into the crisp afternoon air, bags in

both hands, she paused outside the mall entrance. The parking lot glimmered under the sun, and her reflection flashed across the window beside her. She felt so much better after shopping and knew that the day would only get better.

Chapter Four

Brielle drove with the music playing and a smile on her face. It was as if a huge weight had been lifted off her shoulders. She no longer gave a damn what Delano wanted to do. If he didn't want to be in their child's life, he didn't have to be, but nothing was going to stop her from having her baby. Coming to a stop at a red light, Brielle looked over at a Mexican restaurant that had a sign in the window for two-dollar street tacos. Feeling hungry after her day of shopping, Brielle turned the corner and pulled into the parking lot.

Walking inside the restaurant, her nose was filled with the smell of seasoned meats and fresh tortillas. She was seated in seconds and ordered a water with lemon before looking over the menu. She decided on three steak tacos. As she waited on her food, she decided to finally check her phone. She hadn't looked at it since the day before, mainly because she didn't want to read or hear what Delano had to say. Brielle took a sip of her water, as she turned on her phone and waited for it to boot up. She took a deep breath, as her phone chimed constantly, alerting her of the many missed calls and texts she knew were all from Delano.

When her phone was finally done chiming, Brielle looked through her missed calls first. Just as she thought, six of the missed calls were from Delano, two were from her mother, and twenty-five were from her best friend, Amya. She was just about to listen to her voicemail when her food arrived. She placed her phone on the table and poured hot sauce and lime juice on her tacos before taking a bite. Her phone rang just as she took another bite. Looking down at her screen, she saw Amya's face flashing across her display. Wiping her hands on her napkin, she picked up her phone and swiped the talk button.

"Hey, girl, what up doe?"

"Brielle, where the hell have you been? I've been calling you for hours, and you ain't been answering. Bitch, I've texted and left voicemail after voicemail."

"My bad, girl. I had a hard night and decided to take myself shopping to make me feel better. I just turned my phone on. What's up?"

"Bri, I need you to come down to Oakwood Main. Ms. Denise had a heart attack last night. It's bad, Bri."

Brielle grabbed her chest at the mention of heart attack and her mother in the same sentence. "Oh, my God, Amya. I'm on my way right now. Text me her room number."

Brielle's chair scraped against the floor, as she jumped up. Her heart started hammering so hard it felt like it was trying to claw its way out of her chest. She stammered, grabbing her coat and purse with trembling hands. The waiter called after her, letting her know that she hadn't paid for her food yet. But Brielle was already pushing through the door, the blast of cold air hitting her like a slap to the face.

Her mind raced, as she hurried across the parking lot. *My mama had a heart attack?* The words didn't make sense. Her mother was strong and young, barely in her fifties. She still worked full-time, still cooked Sunday dinners like clockwork, and still lived her life. She was too young to have a heart attack.

"No," Brielle mumbled to herself, as she fumbled for her car keys, trying to unlock her door.

Her hands shook so bad she dropped the keys twice before finally unlocking the door. Her breathing was uneven, coming in short, shallow bursts. She slid behind the wheel, slammed the door shut, and took a second to steady herself, but the tears had already started to fall.

"Please, God," she whispered, wiping her cheeks. "Please don't let nothing happen to my mama. Please."

She started the car, throwing it into reverse, before she'd even fastened her seatbelt. Panic pulsed through her veins. Every red light felt like an enemy. Every slow car in front of her made her want to scream. Her mind flashed with memories of her mama teaching her how to braid and laughing in the kitchen while frying chicken. Even yelling at her to stop talking back when she was a teenager. She couldn't lose that. She couldn't lose her.

As she sped down Greenfield, tears blurred her vision. She swiped at her eyes with the back of her hand, muttering, "Come on, come on, please come on," every time the light turned yellow. When the light finally turned green again, Brielle pressed the gas, and the phone that was sitting in her lap slid to the floor. She cursed, reaching for it without thinking. Before Brielle could do anything, the sound of screeching tires filled the air right before the blinding flash of headlights. Then, there was the deafening sound of metal against metal.

Her body jerked forward, the seatbelt snapping tight across her chest. The sound was brutal – glass shattering, horns blaring, and the world spinning. Then, silence. For a second, all Brielle could hear was her heartbeat – fast, frantic, and uneven. The airbag had exploded in front of her, and smoke and powder filled the car. Her head throbbed, her chest ached, and confusion clouded her mind. She tried to move, but her body didn't cooperate.

"No, no, no," she gasped, voice breaking. "I gotta get to my mama."

A sharp pain shot through her stomach. Instinctively, she touched it. "My baby..."

Her eyes darted to the cracked windshield, to the faint shape of another car in front of her, a black Range Rover, smoke curling from its hood. She heard a door slam then heavy footsteps. Then, a man's voice shouted, "Hey! You okay?!"

The driver of the other car was already running toward her. He yanked her door handle, cursing when it didn't open.

"Hold on," he assured, his voice low but urgent. "Don't move. You got hit hard, my baby."

Brielle blinked up at him through tears, her mind spinning. The man's face came into focus. She saw his dark skin, sharp jawline, and beard that was neatly trimmed. His eyes were steady, locked on hers, filled with concern instead of anger.

"I-I gotta get to the hospital," she stammered, trying to unbuckle her seatbelt. "My mama..."

He gently placed his hand on her shoulder through the broken window.. "That's where you're going, to the hospital. You might be hurt. Lemme call 911," he spoke calmly.

"I can't wait," Brielle cried. "I gotta go. Please."

He crouched beside the door, his tone softening. "Listen. You gon' get there, aight? But you gotta breathe first. Calm down, my baby, and just take a few deep breaths."

Something about his voice, both deep and grounding, cut through her panic. She nodded weakly, her hands shaking as he dialed for help. The minutes that followed blurred together. Sirens in the distance, flashing blue and red lights, and all Brielle could think about was her mother. Brielle sat there, trembling, half in shock, half in disbelief, clutching her stomach, as tears streamed down her face.

When the paramedics arrived, their voices echoed around her. The car door was cut open, and strong hands lifted her out carefully. As they laid her on the stretcher, her eyes found the man who'd helped her. He was standing near the curb, hands in his pockets now, watching her with quiet concern.

"Take me to Oakwood Main. My mama's there."

The paramedic nodded, checking her vitals. "We're headed there anyway."

The moment the gurney was wheeled into the hospital room, Brielle's voice cracked through the air. "I'm pregnant," she blurted, breath shaky, as she tried to sit up. "Please-please make sure my baby's okay. And my mama. She was brought in last night. They said she had a heart attack. Her name is Denise Robinson. Can somebody please tell me if she's okay?"

Her words came out in a rush. One nurse, a woman with soft brown eyes and a deep brown skin tone, pressed a gentle hand against Brielle's arm.

"Sweetheart, we're going to check on your mom as soon as we make sure you and your baby are okay, alright?"

Brielle nodded weakly, her bottom lip trembling. Her heart still hadn't slowed down since the crash, and now the fear of what she might've done to her baby was twisting inside her chest like a knife. They wheeled her into a small exam room that was filled with bright lights. The smell of antiseptic hit her nose, sharp and sterile, replacing the faint sweetness of her perfume. She wanted to scream, to cry, to get up and run down the hallway until she found her mama's room, but her body wouldn't let her.

Her hands lay folded over her stomach, as a nurse clipped monitors onto her fingers and wrist. The steady beep of the machine filled the silence, taunting her.

"Your blood pressure's up," the nurse murmured, glancing at the monitor. "You've been through a lot today, so that's understandable."

Brielle just stared at the ceiling, her voice barely above a whisper. "I just... I just need to know my baby's okay so that I can get to my mama."

A few minutes later, the doctor walked in, a tall, older, white man with a calm but serious energy that immediately took over the room.

"Miss Robinson," he spoke gently, glancing down at her chart, "I understand you were in an accident tonight and that you're pregnant. We're going to do an ultrasound to check for any internal injuries and make sure everything looks normal with the baby, okay?"

Brielle nodded, trying to stay still, but her leg bounced nervously beneath the thin hospital blanket.

"Is this your first pregnancy?" he asked.

"Yes," she whispered.

"Alright. Let's take a look."

The nurse helped her adjust, lowering the blanket and pulling her hospital gown up just enough to expose her stomach. The cool gel made her flinch, and she gasped softly as the doctor pressed the ultrasound wand against her skin. The room fell quiet except for the faint hum of the machine. Brielle stared at the screen, tears welling in her eyes before she even knew what she was looking for. Her mind ran wild with every possible fear. She prayed that she hadn't hurt her baby in the crash.

Suddenly, a flicker of sound filled the room. It was the heartbeat, her baby's heartbeat. Brielle smiled as she looked over at the monitor.

"That's your baby," the doctor said softly, a small smile tugging at his lips. "Nice, strong heartbeat. Everything looks good."

Brielle's hand flew to her mouth. A sob escaped her before she could stop it. "Oh, my God..."

The doctor pointed to the small shape on the screen. "You're about eight weeks along, so two months. The baby's measuring right on track. No bleeding and no signs of distress."

"Two months?" Brielle whispered, staring at the little shape on the screen.

She couldn't believe she was already two months along. Her baby was strong already and had survived a lot in a short time. She reached out and brushed her fingertips across the screen like she could touch the heartbeat itself. "Thank you," she whispered, her words trembling. "Thank you, God."

The doctor wiped away the gel and helped her sit up slowly. "You're going to be fine, Miss Robinson. We'll keep you a little while longer for observation, but your vitals are stabilizing. After that, I'll have someone check on your mother's condition for you."

"Please," Brielle replied quickly, clutching the edge of the blanket. "Can you make sure she knows I'm here? If she's awake, I don't want her to worry."

"I'll make sure of it," he assured her before stepping out.

Left alone, Brielle stared at the small black-and-white printout the nurse handed her. A grainy image of the life growing inside her. The tears came again, quieter this time. Relief mixed with exhaustion and heartbreak tangled with gratitude. She pressed the photo against her chest and whispered, "It's just me and you, little one, and we gon' be okay."

Minutes passed before a nurse returned with a small smile. "Your mother's stable," she spoke softly. "They have her in the cardiac unit. She's resting, but you can see her once we finish monitoring you for another hour or so, okay?"

Brielle nodded, tears blurring her vision again. "Thank you."

As the nurse left, she leaned her head back against the pillow, closing her eyes. Her baby was going to be fine, and so was her mother, and all Brielle could do was thank God for his blessings.

Chapter Five

Taj didn't even remember making the decision to follow the ambulance. One second, he was standing in the middle of Greenfield with his heart still pounding from the crash. The next, he was back in his truck, headlights cutting through the darkening sky, following the red and white blur, as it weaved through traffic. Something about the woman inside, her face, her trembling voice when she said, *"my mama,"* stuck with him. He'd been in accidents before, but this one was different. She looked terrified, not just for herself but for her mother.

The hospital parking lot was half-empty when he pulled in. The rain that had started after the crash left the pavement glistening under the yellow lights. Taj sat for a minute, engine idling, trying to convince himself to leave. *You don't even know that girl,* he told himself. *You did your part, and she's safe now. Go home.* But instead of putting the truck in reverse, he turned it off and walked inside.

The waiting room was quiet except for the buzz of the vending machine and a security guard half-dozing behind a counter. The smell of disinfectant hung in the air, mixed with the faint scent of burnt coffee. Taj dropped into one of the plastic chairs and rubbed his face, still feeling the tension in his shoulders. He wasn't even supposed to be out today. He'd planned to chill and relax around the house. However, when his sister called and said that her sink was leaking and her husband was out of town, he knew he had to go over there. He was just supposed to be going to get a burger before he headed home. That was it. Instead, he ended up on the side of the road with a busted taillight and some woman's car smashed into the back of his Range Rover. He should've been mad. But all he wanted to know was if she was okay.

Hours passed, and Taj had gotten up twice to stretch his legs and once to grab a water from the vending machine. His phone buzzed a few times, texts from his friend wanting to know if he wanted to have a few beers. He texted back quickly, telling him he was tied up at the moment and would text him tomorrow, before sliding his phone back into his pocket. He watched the double doors, as he waited for her to walk through them. He didn't know her name, so he knew walking up to the information desk wouldn't do him any good. So, all he could do was wait.

Around ten that night, the automatic doors slid open. Taj looked up and froze when he saw her. She was moving slowly, wrapped in a thin hospital blanket, with her long, blonde braids spilling over her shoulder. Her eyes looked tired, red from crying, but she was standing and walking out the hospital, so Taj knew everything was good. Beside her was another woman, tall and brown-skinned, with her arm around her shoulders. They talked quietly as they walked, but Taj couldn't hear what they were saying. He just watched the way she held her stomach protectively, the way her shoulders sagged with exhaustion but still held grace. Something about her hit him in a place he didn't know existed.

He stood up before he even realized it, running a hand down his beard as if to straighten himself out. He'd been sitting for hours, still in the black hoodie and jeans he'd thrown on earlier, and suddenly, he was aware of how rough he probably looked. Still, he couldn't let her walk out without saying something. He crossed the waiting room in slow, steady steps, the sound of his

Timbs echoing off the tile. The friend noticed him first, pausing mid-sentence.

"Can we help you?" she asked, cautious but not rude.

Taj's eyes didn't leave Brielle. "I just wanted to make sure you were straight," he announced, his voice deep but calm. "You the one from the accident, right?"

Brielle blinked, surprise flickering in her eyes. "Yeah, and I'm fine. Thanks for asking."

He nodded once, offering a small, genuine smile. "I'm Taj. I was in the Range Rover."

Brielle's eyes widened. "Oh, my God. You're the guy that I hit. I'm so sorry. Are you okay? Have you been here all this time?"

"Yeah, I stayed to make sure you were okay. I didn't know your name, so I couldn't ask anyone. I just had to wait until you walked out."

"It's Brielle, and you didn't have to do that. I'm fine. Thank you so much. We should probably exchange information, so we can get our insurance companies involved, huh?" Brielle reached into her purse and pulled out her phone. "What's your number?"

Taj gave Brielle his number before saving hers in his phone. He told her that he would reach out to her in the next couple of days. Brielle nodded, and he watched as she walked out the hospital. Taj walked to his truck, pulling out the parking lot, and headed home. He knew her car was totaled, and because of the accident being her fault, he knew that she would be the one that would have to pay for everything. Taj didn't want that. So, he decided that when he did reach out to her, he would tell her that he would cover his own damages.

Chapter Six

The next morning, the light creeping through Brielle's blinds was far too bright for how she felt. Her entire body ached. Her shoulders were stiff, neck sore, and her thighs burned every time she moved. She groaned as she sat up slowly, wincing when her ribs protested. Yesterday's accident replayed in her head like a loop she couldn't pause – the screech of tires, the flash of headlights, and the jolt that had knocked her breath away. But she was alive. Her baby was alive. That was all that mattered.

She took her time getting dressed, slipping into a loose-fitting cream sweatsuit, before putting on her shoes. Every movement reminded her that her body had been through something traumatic, but she refused to let it stop her. Her mother was still in the hospital, and she wasn't about to let pain keep her away. Brielle requested an Uber and sat on her couch, while she waited for it to arrive.

Ten minutes later, she was in the backseat of a Ford Explorer, heading to the hospital. She placed her AirPods into her ears, and SZA's *Good Days* played. Yesterday had changed everything. Between the accident, finding out exactly how far along she was, and seeing her mother laid up in that hospital bed, Brielle felt like she'd been shaken awake from a life she didn't recognize anymore.

When she walked into her mother's hospital room, she froze

for a second. Denise looked better than she had the night before. Her color was back, her breathing even, and her hair wrapped neatly in a silk scarf like she was at home. Most importantly, she was alert and talking, ten times better than the way she was when Brielle saw her yesterday. But seeing her mother like that, connected to machines and IVs, still hit her hard.

"Hey, baby girl," Denise rasped with a tired smile when she saw her. "You look like you been through hell."

Brielle forced a shaky laugh, as she stepped closer. "You're one to talk." She leaned down and kissed her mother's forehead gently then pulled a chair closer to the bed. "How you feeling, Ma?"

Denise sighed, glancing toward the monitors beside her. "Better than yesterday. They say it was a mild heart attack. I scared myself, but I guess God wasn't done with me yet."

Brielle's throat tightened. "You can't be doing that, Ma. You gotta start taking care of yourself. Eating better and exercising regularly. You scared the hell out of me, Ma."

Her mother gave a weak chuckle. "Girl, you sound like you the mama."

"I'm being serious," Brielle uttered, blinking back tears. "I can't... I can't lose you. Especially not now."

Denise tilted her head, studying her daughter's face. "What you mean, especially not now? You bet not want to lose me at all."

Brielle's hands trembled in her lap. She hadn't planned on telling her this way, sitting in a hospital room with her hooked up to monitors. But it felt wrong to keep it to herself any longer.

She took a slow breath. "Ma... I'm pregnant."

Denise's eyes widened, the shock visible even through her exhaustion. "Pregnant? Baby, are you serious?"

Brielle nodded, her eyes filling with tears she couldn't hold back this time. "Yeah. I found out a few weeks ago."

"I'm gonna be a glam ma? Oh, my God, this is the best news I've gotten all day. I can't wait to spoil that baby. I know Delano is excited. What did he say? Does he want a boy or a girl? He probably wants a boy for his first child, huh?"

Brielle's smile quickly faded, as she thought about Delano's reaction to her pregnancy. She didn't want to tell her mother about Delano and add on any more stress to her, but Brielle's face told it all.

"What's wrong, baby girl?" Denise asked.

"Nothing, Ma. I'm fine. I'm happy about my baby."

"But Delano's not, huh?" Denise spoke, reading her daughter's face.

"He tried to give me money for an abortion, but I didn't take it. He says he doesn't want to be a father."

For a moment, the room was silent except for the steady beep of the heart monitor. Then, Denise reached out and grabbed Brielle's hand, her grip surprisingly firm.

"Then he don't deserve to be one. You hear me? If he don't want to step up, that's on him. But that baby is a blessing, Brielle. Don't let nobody make you feel otherwise."

Brielle sniffled, a tear slipping down her cheek. "I know this baby is a blessin', Ma. It's just... I didn't expect to be doing it alone."

Denise squeezed her hand again. "You're not alone. You got me, and you know I'ma be there to help you with my grandbaby. You and that baby gon' be good, you understand me?"

Brielle smiled through the tears that fell from her eyes. "You should be worrying about making sure you good first."

Denise chuckled, the sound raspy but warm. "Don't worry 'bout me. I got motivation now. Gotta be here to see my grandbaby."

Brielle smiled before leaning in and kissing her mother on the forehead. She stayed by Denise's side for hours. She told her about the ultrasound and how she'd seen that tiny flicker of a heartbeat on the screen. Brielle was at peace with the decision she made to keep her baby. With her mother by her side, she knew she would be able to do anything.

It was around six that evening when Denise finally forced Brielle to go home. She stood in the hospital lobby, as she waited on her Uber to arrive. Her phone vibrated in her hand, and the name Taj flashed across her screen.

"Hello?" she answered softly.

"Hey," a deep voice answered after a pause. His tone was calm and steady. "It's Taj. How are you today?"

Brielle exhaled, her shoulders sagging just a little. "Oh... hey. I'm so glad you called." Her voice cracked on the words, and she swallowed quickly, trying to sound composed. "I wanted to reach out, but I didn't even know where to start."

Taj chuckled lightly but not unkindly. "Yeah, it turned out to be a crazy night."

"Crazy doesn't even begin to describe it." Brielle rubbed her temple, guilt swirling in her chest all over again. "I'm really sorry, Taj. About everything. I wasn't paying attention like I should've been. I was just..." She stopped, biting her lip before continuing. "I was in a rush trying to get to my mom. I found out she was brought into the hospital after having a heart attack, and I wasn't thinking straight. I shouldn't have been behind the wheel like that."

There was silence on the other end for a moment. Then, Taj spoke, his tone softer than before. "I get it. You were scared. I would have been too. How is she doing?"

"She's doing much better. Thank you for asking."

"That's good," Taj replied.

A long pause stretched between them before Brielle spoke again.

"I know you're calling for my insurance information, but I'm leaving the hospital and about to get into an Uber. Would you mind if I called you back in about thirty minutes once I'm home?"

"I was actually calling to tell you not to worry about it."

Brielle blinked. "What do you mean don't worry about it?"

"I'll take care of it myself. You don't need to go through your insurance. You already got enough on your plate."

She frowned, confused. "Taj, I hit you, so this is my responsibility."

"I know," he replied, his tone calm but firm. "But it's not that deep. The damage wasn't that bad, and I'll get it fixed. Besides, I saw your car, and you're going to need a new one."

Brielle stared out at the street in disbelief, her lips parting slightly. People didn't just do things like that, not in her world. Most folks would've been angry and demanding, waiting to get a check out of her. But here this man was, someone she didn't even know, telling her not to worry about it like it was nothing.

Her heart gave a strange flutter. "Taj, I appreciate that. I really do. But I don't feel right letting you do that."

"It's already done. Look, things happen. I can tell you're a good person. I was just in the wrong place at the wrong time."

She was quiet for a long moment, not knowing exactly what to say. "Thank you," she finally spoke, her voice soft. "You didn't have to do that."

"I know, but I wanted to."

Brielle exhaled slowly, her shoulders relaxing. "Still, I'm sorry about the accident."

"Hey, it's fine. I'm telling you. The most important thing is that you're okay and that you got to your mother, and she's okay. A car can be replaced. People can't."

"Yeah, I guess you're right about that."

When her Uber pulled up outside, Brielle glanced through the glass doors. "My Uber just pulled up. However, if you're not going to let me pay for your car, at least allow me to take you to lunch or something. I just feel like I need to repay you somehow."

"You don't gotta thank me. But if you insist, then I'm never gon' turn down a meal." Taj chuckled.

"Great, how 'bout Tuesday afternoon? I'll text you the time and place."

"Sounds good. I'll be there."

With that, Brielle ended the call and got into her Uber. The fifteen minute ride back to her house was quiet. She watched in the window at the streetlight and the houses decorated for

Halloween. When the driver pulled up to her house, she thanked him and got out the car. She walked as fast as her body allowed her, attempting to get out the cold as quickly as possible. Walking inside her house, she locked the door behind her, took off her coat, and went right up to her bathroom.

Brielle began running herself a bath before pouring in some lavender scented bubble bath. She then lit several candles around the bathroom before finally grabbing her phone and laptop and placing them onto her bath shelf. After taking off her clothes, she eased down into the tub and let the warmth of the water surround her body. She found a movie on Netflix and relaxed.

About fifteen minutes into her soak, her phone rang. Thinking it was her mother, Brielle quickly set up, her body protesting the moment she moved. She sighed heavily when she looked at her screen and saw Delano's face flashing across it. *What the fuck does he want?* Brielle thought, as she swiped the talk button.

"Hello?"

"What you doing, and where you at?" Delano asked.

"Delano, what do you want? Let's not pretend that we are even cool right now."

"You at home? I want to see you," Delano replied, completely ignoring Brielle's last statement.

"Yes, I'm at my house, but that don't mean you will be here. I don't want to see you."

"If I want to come there, I will. Don't forget that I'm the one that pays the rent on that muthafucka, so you can even stay there. So, don't tell me where I can't be. I see you still actin' mad. Why don't you stop that shit and embrace me lovingly? I'm tryna fuck with you, my baby."

"You tryna fuck with me just not the kid growin' inside of me, huh?"

"See, you still on that shit, Brielle. I told you to take care of that shit, and things could go right back to normal. We was happy before you walked into my loft and told me that bullshit. Get rid of the bullshit, and we can go back to being happy."

"Delano, why are you calling me? I've already told you I'm keeping my baby. If you don't want to be a part of his or her life, then that's on you!"

"Fine, if this is the game you want to play, then that's on you."

Before Brielle could say another word, Delano hung up. Brielle shook her head and placed her phone back onto her bath shelf. She didn't understand why he'd even called her. She laid back in the tub and finished her movie. When she got out, Brielle made herself something to eat before relaxing on the couch for the rest of the night.

Chapter Seven

Brielle sat in one of the uncomfortable chairs by the nurses' station, scrolling absently through her phone, as she waited for her mother to be discharged. It was Monday morning, and after spending the entire weekend in the hospital, Brielle knew her mother was more than ready to get home.

"Girl! Why the fuck are hospitals always so damn cold? And why the fuck they takin' so long? A bitch needs to get to some heat. You know my blood low," Amya announced, as she strutted through the automatic doors, hips swaying in her jeans and fur-trimmed denim jacket. Her long, jet-black hair was bone straight and parted down the middle. She'd gone down to the coffee shop on the lower level to grab them both a latte.

Brielle couldn't help but laugh, as she took the coffee cup from Amya. "Nobody told you to come in here tryna catch a doctor. It's cold outside, so you knew it would be cold in here," she teased, eyeing Amya's outfit.

"Listen," Amya spoke, taking a sip of her latte, "you never know who you might run into. There's doctors, nurses, security guards. Somebody's son gon' be fine up in here."

"Girl, this is not *Grey's Anatomy*. This is Oakwood Main. You won't be *Married to Medicine* out this muthafucka."

"Mmm," Amya hummed dramatically. "Well, it should be. I could use a McDreamy."

Before Brielle could reply, the door to her mother's room opened, and Denise appeared, being rolled out in a wheelchair. She was dressed in a cozy sweatsuit, her hair pulled back neatly, and she had a full face of makeup. Even after a heart attack, Denise Robinson was going to make sure she looked good when she stepped outside.

"Hey, Mama," Brielle greeted, walking over to her. Relief washed through her seeing her mother up and moving. "You look so much better."

"I feel so much better," Denise replied, smiling. "I told them I didn't need this wheelchair, but they acting like I can't walk up outta here. I'm just happy I'm finally going home. I'm ready to get into my own bed." Her eyes shifted to Amya. "Oh, and my bonus daughter came out to see me too? I can't believe it."

"Hey, Mama D!" Amya grinned, rushing over and leaning down to hug her. "You scared the hell outta us, you know that? You knew damn well I was going to come get you from the hospital."

"Shit, I scared my damn self. I gotta stop fuckin' with them YNs. That dick damn near took a bitch out."

"Ma!" Brielle yelled, looking over at her mother.

Denise burst out laughing. "Girl, you know I'm just playin'. Calm yo' ass down."

Brielle shook her head before grabbing the small duffel bag that sat on Denise's lap, along with a stack of discharge papers. Amya told the nurse that she could take over the wheelchair and wheel Denise out herself. The nurse smiled before stepping aside. Once they got outside, Amya helped Denise into her car, while Brielle placed her things into the trunk. Once they were all in the car, Amya looked at Denise through her rearview mirror.

"What you wanna listen to, Mama D?" Amya asked.

"Put on some K Dot."

"See, this why we get along." Amya smiled, putting on *Euphoria* and turning up the volume before pulling off.

Denise bobbed her head to the beat before speaking. "Lord, it feels good to be out of there. I swear, if I heard one more machine beep, I was gonna unplug my damn self."

Amya cackled. "Not *unplug yourself,* Mama D. Stop playin'."

"Shit, who playin'? That shit was getting on my damn nerves. And I need some real food. That nasty ass hospital food was gon' make me sicker than I already was."

"Girl, we gon' get you right," Amya assured, as she merged onto I-94. "I'm gonna make a pot of chili tonight. You want me to bring you a bowl?"

"Only if you using ground beef," Denise warned. "That fake meat you be eatin' taste like sadness and a struggle that I ain't never had."

Brielle laughed so hard she nearly spilled her coffee. "Mama!"

"What? I said what I said. That shit be nasty as hell, and you know it too. And why yo' ass look so tired? You ain't get no sleep last night?"

"I'm okay, Mama," Brielle said softly, glancing out the window. "Just glad you're alright. That's all that matters."

For a brief moment, Denise just looked at her daughter. "Yeah, okay, yo' ass gon' tell me what's wrong with you. It don't have to be now, but you're going to tell me."

Amya looked over at Brielle. "You good for real, sis?"

Brielle hesitated. "I'm... I'm gon' be okay. It's just a lot going on right now, but I'ma be good. I just gotta stay positive."

Amya nodded knowingly. "Translation, you been crying every other day."

Brielle rolled her eyes. "Mind your business."

"Girl, your business *is* my business," Amya revealed. "You think just 'cause you didn't tell me about Delano I ain't know? Please. I knew something was off the second you started posting all them quote memes a couple weeks ago."

Denise chuckled. "The 'God, remove anyone not meant for me' ones?"

"*Exactly!*" Amya snapped her fingers, laughing. "Soon as I saw that one, I said, 'Oh, she going through it.'"

Brielle covered her face, laughing despite herself. "Y'all are too much. Please stop."

Denise smiled faintly, her voice turning soft. "I told you that you and the baby are gon' be good. Fuck that nigga. You don't need him. You can't make no nigga be a father, so please don't try."

Brielle nodded her head slowly. "I know, Mama. I just still can't believe he's acting like this."

"Hold up, bitch. What baby? You pregnant?" Amya asked.

"Yeah, I'm sorry. I know I should have told you. I found out a few weeks ago, and it's just been a lot going on since then. When I got into the accident the other day, I found out that I was two months. Delano tried to give me five thousand dollars to have an abortion. I didn't take it though."

"First off, you should have took that money. You could have bought the baby a lot of shit with that. Secondly, I can't believe I'm about to be a god mommy. I can't wait. You don't need that nigga. We got you and that baby. You know that," Amya reassured.

"That's the same thing I said. My daughter and grandchild will always be okay as long as I got breath in my body."

"Says the woman who just had a heart attack." Brielle chuckled.

Amya and Denise burst out laughing. When they made it to Denise's house, Amya parked in her driveway, and they all got out the car with Brielle grabbing her bag from the trunk.

Once they got her inside and settled on the couch, Denise sighed contently. "Home sweet home. I can't wait to take me a good ass shower and get me something to eat. I want some Chinese so bad."

"You need anything before we go?" Brielle asked, looking over at her mother.

"No, I'm good, baby. Once I get out the shower, I'm going to order my food and sit on my couch and enjoy my first night back at home," Denise revealed.

"What about the chili I'm cookin'?"

"I told you I don't want none of that shit. Are you tryna put me back in the hospital for eating fake meat?"

"I don't know what you think Chinese food is, but that shit ain't real. You go ahead and eat that shit though. I'll enjoy my chili myself," Amya said, rolling her eyes.

Brielle laughed before kissing her mother goodbye, and the two walked out the door. When Amya pulled up to Brielle's house about fifteen minutes later, she asked Brielle if she wanted her to come inside, but Brielle declined, letting her know that she was going to take a nap and would call her later. Amaya agreed, and Brielle walked inside and went directly to her room. Her mother was right. After Delano's call last night, she'd barely gotten any sleep and was about to make up for it. Peeling out of her clothes, Brielle got into bed, put the covers over her head, and got all the sleep that she hadn't gotten the night before.

When Brielle finally woke up, it was a little after five in the evening. She rolled out of bed and used the bathroom before heading to her kitchen to fix herself something to eat. After making a grilled chicken salad, she sat at the table to eat her food. She decided to use that time to scroll through TikTok to find a nice restaurant to take Taj to for her apology lunch. After scrolling through several videos, Brielle decided on Townhouse and shot a text to Taj, asking him if he could meet her there at two tomorrow. When he agreed, Brielle finished her salad and curled up on the couch with a cup of tea and a book.

BRIELLE BEGAN GETTING DRESSED about twelve the following afternoon. The wind rattled the windows, and a light dusting of snow covered the ground. She knew it was cold outside; however, she still wanted to look cute. Her mother had taught Brielle at an early age to never look like what she was going through. So, the ache in her heart would never show through the reflection in the mirror.

She chose a soft beige turtleneck that she paired with high-waisted, dark denim jeans that sculpted her hips and thighs, tucking neatly into a pair of caramel colored knee-high leather boots. Brielle slid her gold hoop earrings into her ears then reached for her jewelry box. She fastened a dainty gold chain around her neck, a gift from her mother a couple years ago on her twenty-first birthday, before reaching for her fragrance of choice. Today, it would be Kayali Vanilla Royale Sugared Patchouli 64. It was the perfect fragrance to wear on a cold day.

She looked at herself once more in the mirror before applying gloss to her lips. She fixed her baby hairs and was ready to go. She grabbed her purse and went into the living room to wait for her Uber. Once in the car, she shot a text to Taj letting him know that she was on her way.

Taj was already at the restaurant when Brielle walked up to the hostess stand. The glass walls glowed softly with warm yellow lighting, and from the outside, she could see him sitting at a high-top near the window. He spotted her as soon as she stepped inside. He stood, nodding his head toward her when they locked eyes.

Taj wore a black crewneck sweater that clung to his chest and arms just enough to show he was solid underneath. His jeans were dark, fitted but not tight, cuffed neatly over wheat-colored ACG boots. A fresh line-up framed his face, and his full beard looked soft and was tapered perfectly around a sharp jawline.

"Hey," Brielle greeted when she reached the table, trying not to stare too hard.

"Hey there," Taj replied, his voice deep yet gentle. "I got us a table. I hope that's cool with you."

"It's perfect." Brielle slipped out of her coat and draped it over the chair. As she sat down, the waitress came over to drop off menus and water. After she left, a quiet moment settled between them, a little awkward but not uncomfortable.

"So..." Brielle smiled faintly. "I'm glad you made it."

"I wasn't gonna miss out on a free lunch." He leaned back in his seat. "Plus, I wanted to make sure you were really okay after the accident. You look much better."

"Thanks. I feel better."

They started with small talk, easy conversation, the weather, the holidays that were coming up, the decorations already going up downtown. It was all generic and safe, yet Brielle found herself relaxing faster than she expected. After a while, she cleared her throat.

"Taj... I really want to apologize again for the accident. I should've been more careful. This could have ended way worse than it did. I'm just glad it didn't."

He shook his head, smiling a little. "It's cool, Brielle, really. If anything, I should be thanking you."

She blinked. "Thanking me?"

"Yeah." His eyes held hers. "I got to meet you."

Brielle's breath caught for a second. It wasn't slick or rehearsed; he sounded honest. His tone, his smile, the way he looked at her, she could tell he was flirting. And she couldn't pretend she didn't notice.

"That's sweet," she smiled, "but... I should probably tell you something."

Taj straightened a little, giving her his full attention.

"I'm pregnant," Brielle spoke. "Two months."

His eyebrows lifted, not in shock, more like surprise. However, his expression stayed warm. "Oh." He nodded slowly. "Thank you for telling me." He rubbed the back of his neck, his voice softening. "I'm sorry. I didn't know you were in a relationship."

"I'm not," she insisted. "It's... complicated."

Their eyes held for a moment. Taj nodded again, this time with understanding. "Got you."

Before either of them could say anything else, the waitress returned. "You guys ready to order?"

Brielle exhaled, grateful for the interruption. "Yeah, I'll have the chicken and waffle sliders please."

"And I'll take the short rib grilled cheese," Taj ordered, handing over his menu. "Extra pickles on the side."

The waitress smiled. "You got it."

Once she walked away, conversation picked back up. Taj didn't pry about the pregnancy. He didn't ask who the father was or what "complicated" meant. Instead, he talked to her like he had before she'd even told him. They laughed over funny stories they shared with each other and had an all-around good time. Brielle found herself laughing more at lunch than she had in the past few weeks.

When their food came, they kept talking between bites, the conversation flowing smoothly. Two hours passed before either of them realized how long they'd been sitting there.

When the waitress came to drop off the bill, Taj automatically reached for it. "I got it."

Brielle shook her head, already pulling her wallet from her purse. "No. This was my idea. My apology, my olive branch, my check."

"Brielle..."

"Nope." She slid her card out. "Don't argue with me. I asked you to lunch."

He laughed softly. "Alright. If you insist."

"And I do."

The waitress was back with Brielle's card moments later, handing it back to her with a warm smile. Taj held the door open, as they stepped out of Townhouse Detroit, the cold November air slapping across their faces. He headed toward the parking lot, hitting his key fob and sounding off his alarm. Brielle stayed planted by the front entrance, tugging her coat tighter around herself.

Taj turned around halfway to his truck, eyebrows pulling together. "Brielle... what you doin'? What you waitin' on?"

"An Uber," she replied. "Should only take a few minutes."

He stared at her as if what she said was the craziest thing he'd ever heard. "Nah. Hell nah." He shook his head, walking back toward her. "Ain't no way you 'bout to get in an Uber after leaving anywhere with me. Come on. I'm takin' you home."

"Taj..."

"Don't argue with me," he spoke low, gentle yet firm. "You

pregnant. It's cold as hell out here, and you wanna stand out here and wait for a stranger to pick you up. Nah, I'm right here, and I got you."

"Okay," she finally murmured and followed him to his truck.

He opened the passenger door for her, waited until she was buckled, then got in and pulled up his GPS.

"What's your address?"

She gave it to him and watched as he typed it in. The ride was quiet but not awkward. When they turned onto her block, Brielle saw the car parked in front of her house but thought nothing of it. That was until they pulled into her driveway. There was a man standing at her front door, taping a piece of paper to the middle of it.

"What the hell?" she whispered.

Taj put the car in park but didn't cut the engine. His eyes followed hers, as he looked over at the man. Brielle unbuckled quickly and jumped out of the truck.

"Excuse me!" she called, walking fast toward the man. "Who are you? And what are you putting on my door?"

He turned around, holding a clipboard, looking stone faced. "Ma'am, I'm with the property management company. This is an eviction notice."

"Eviction?" She laughed even though nothing was funny. "No. That's not right at all. My rent gets paid every month, and it was for sure paid this month. So, I'm sure that eviction notice is a mistake."

"This eviction notice is not for non-payment," he spoke, tapping his clipboard. "Your lease was month-to-month. The owner has chosen not to renew. You have thirty days to vacate the property."

"Month-to-month? What are you talking about? This is a five-year lease, and I'm not even finished with year one," she snapped. "I have the lease I signed right inside my house. I can go get it."

"Ma'am, there's no need for that. I have a copy of your lease right here. Like I said, you have thirty days to vacate."

"Sir, you cannot just throw me out of my home."

"I see this happen every day. Especially with a month-to-month lease like you have. The owner wants to take the property in a different direction."

"I don't have a month-to-month lease! I'm telling you that this is some type of mistake."

"There is no mistake. This is your lease, and as you can see on the first line in bold letters are the words month-to-month."

The man handed Brielle the lease for her to look over. Her eyes darted to the words in bold, just as the man said. Her address was next. Then, when she flipped to the next page and saw Delano's signature, her heart dropped. However, before she could say anything, Taj stepped up.

"Is everything alright?"

Brielle's chest heaved, as she continued to look down at the lease she'd never seen before. She wanted to cry but knew that wouldn't change her situation. Instead, Brielle nodded her head.

"Yes, everything is fine. Thank you so much for the ride, Taj," Brielle lied.

"Are you sure?" Taj questioned, still looking at the man.

"Yes, I'm sure."

Taj nodded his head before slowly walking back to his car. Brielle, pissed, turned on her heels and stomped up her steps. She couldn't believe that she had been played by Delano yet again. From behind her, she could hear the man telling her that she had thirty days to vacate her home. She snatched the letter from her door before walking inside and slamming the door behind her. Rushing up to her room, she grabbed the lease she'd signed that she now knew was fake.

"This got to be the weakest shit a nigga could ever do. Fuck this shit! He gonna have to answer for this," Brielle spoke out loud, as she looked over the two leases.

With that, Brielle grabbed her phone from her purse, pulled up the Uber app, and ordered an Uber to Delano's loft.

Chapter Eight

When the Uber driver pulled up in front of Delano's building, Brielle thanked him under her breath and got out the car. She walked into the building, anger overflowing inside her. By the time she reached the top floor and turned down the hallway toward his loft, she was ready – ready for an argument, ready for the truth, ready for everything Delano had to say.

The door to Delano's loft was propped open. Three women in matching red Polo shirts were walking out with cleaning supplies and trash bags in hand. Brielle slowed, confusion replacing her irritation. One of the women, a middle-aged lady with gloves still on, smiled politely, as she locked eyes with Brielle.

"Um, excuse me," Brielle murmured, stepping forward. "Is Delano inside?"

The woman blinked at her, puzzled. "I'm sorry, baby... Who?"

"Delano," Brielle repeated, feeling a jolt of impatience. "He's the man that lives here."

Another cleaner came out behind her, dragging a mop bucket. She was quietly singing along to the song playing from her headphones.

The first woman shook her head. "We don't know nobody by that name. We just here to flip the unit."

"Flip it?" Brielle echoed.

"For the next guest," the woman said. "This loft stays booked solid. Maybe because the owner offers long term rentals. The owner don't play about her money."

Brielle's stomach flipped. "I-I'm sorry... booked? Long term rentals? What do you mean?" She stepped closer to the open door, staring into the space she'd been inside just days ago.

"Ma'am, this is an Airbnb. Whoever it was that you said was staying here no longer here. I've been working with the owner for the past five years. She has several properties throughout the city."

Each word stacked on top of the last until they crushed the last piece of denial Brielle had been holding onto. Delano didn't live there; he never did. The fact that he really wasn't the person Brielle thought he was hit her like a ton of bricks. The nights they spent together, the love she thought they had, was a web of lies that had been unraveling since the moment she'd told Delano she was pregnant. Brielle backed away from the doorway as if it was on fire. Her throat tightened, breath thinning, as the truth hit her hard and fast.

"Are you alright, sweetheart?" the cleaning woman asked, her voice gentle.

Brielle nodded automatically, though nothing inside her felt alright. The ground felt like it was tilting. Her chest felt bruised, and humiliation flooded her so fast her face burned.

"Yeah," she managed quietly. "I'm fine."

However, as she walked away, her vision blurred with tears that she didn't want to fall. Every step felt heavier than the last. She had come here ready to confront Delano and get answers about a fake lease, and the entire time, that wasn't the only thing that had been fake.

Brielle's hands were shaking by the time she reached the lobby. She didn't even realize she was walking so fast until she nearly collided with a man stepping out of the elevator. She muttered a quick apology and pushed through the glass doors, desperate for air. The cold November wind slapped her across the face, but it did nothing to cool the burn rising in her chest. She stopped on the sidewalk, pulled out her phone, and hit Delano's name, her thumb trembling over the screen. *He got to explain this shit,* she thought, as she pressed the call button and placed her phone to her ear.

The phone rang once, twice, then a robotic voice clicked on. **"The number you are trying to reach is no longer in service."**

Brielle froze. She pulled the phone away from her ear and stared at the screen as if it had lied to her. As if somehow the lines had been crossed the moment she called the number. She tried again with her heart pounding and her breath shallow. The phone rang twice, then the same voice recording played. Brielle's world seemed to tilt again. Delano had changed his number. He'd called her one last time to tell her to abort their baby, and when she said no, he'd disappeared and took everything Brielle knew with him. For a second, she couldn't breathe at all.

"He really did me like this," she whispered to herself, voice cracking.

Brielle swallowed hard and blinked the tears away. Crying in the middle of downtown wasn't going to help her. Falling apart wasn't going to rewind anything. She needed to get home and think about her next move, but the pain clouded her thoughts. The tears fell just as quickly as she wiped them away.

Finally, she opened the Uber app. A black Hyundai Sonata was four minutes away. She hugged her coat tighter around her waist, fighting against the cold and everything breaking inside her. Brielle stood there alone, feeling the weight of Delano's betrayal sitting heavy on her chest. He had taken away her home. He'd lied about his home. He had left her pregnant and alone. And now, he'd cut off every way she had of reaching him.

As the Uber pulled up to the curb, she took one last glance at the building where she thought her future had been. Then, she squared her shoulders, wiped her face, and forced herself to climb into the backseat.

"Heading home?" the driver asked gently.

"Yeah," Brielle whispered, staring out the window, knowing that even that house wouldn't be hers for long.

By the time the Uber pulled up in front of her house, Brielle felt hollow, like everything inside her had been scraped out until there was nothing left. She unlocked the door with a shaking hand and stepped inside. She dropped her keys on the entry table and went straight to the living room, sinking onto the couch with a heaviness that didn't seem to match her small frame. For a minute, she just sat there, staring at nothing, letting the reality of everything settle like dust around her.

Her chest tightened, as she reached for her phone again. She went to Facebook and typed his name into the search bar. *User not found.* She then went to TikTok. *Account deactivated.* Finally, she checked Snapchat and found that his account was completely gone. Every social media he'd ever had was deleted, completely wiped clean, like he had never existed at all. Her breathing hitched, a sick feeling curling in her stomach. She tossed the phone onto the couch beside her and pressed both hands to her face.

"Why would you do me like this, Delano? Why? I thought you fuckin' loved me."

She leaned back, staring up at the ceiling, as tears pooled in her eyes. For a moment, she held them in, refusing to fall apart. But then, the eviction notice flashed across her mind, the papers shoved in her face earlier. Thirty days to get out of the home she thought would be hers for years to come. A choked sob broke from her chest. Brielle curled onto her side on the couch, one hand instinctively cradling her stomach, as if her body was trying to protect the only thing she had left.

"I'm sorry, baby," she whispered through her tears. "I'm so sorry. I don't know what we're gonna do, but I promise you Mama is going to figure it out."

Her shoulders shook, as she cried, the sound muffled against her arm. She cried for Delano's lies, for the child she was carrying alone, for the eviction notice, for the fear clawing at her throat. And she cried for the future that suddenly looked so dark that she couldn't see through it. She cried until her head hurt and her chest ached. She cried until her eyes were too heavy to keep open, falling asleep right there on her couch.

THE NEXT MORNING, Brielle woke up with her eyes swollen from hours of crying. Her whole face felt tight, and her body felt heavier than usual. For a few seconds, she stayed still, staring up at the ceiling. Then, the reality of everything quickly rushed back to her. A dull ache pressed behind her eyes, but she forced herself to sit up. Crying wasn't going to change anything. She had to move, had to come up with a plan.

She reached for her phone and opened her banking apps. Although Delano had asked her to quit her job a few months ago, promising to take care of her, she had a little money saved up across three different accounts. Altogether, she had a little over six thousand dollars, which was not a lot compared to everything she needed. Her car was done for, and that was something that she needed to get as soon as possible. She knew she couldn't take Ubers every day, and being without a car was not an option.

Brielle got up and took a quick shower. She dressed in a pair of leggings, a black hoodie, and a pair of black Timbs then requested an Uber. The place she ended up at wasn't fancy – just a row of older cars lined up under a faded sign that read **Derrick's Auto Deals.** A sales rep walked her through the options, most of which she knew she couldn't afford. Finally, she settled on a 2012 Chevy Malibu. It had a small dent in the passenger door and over 130,000 miles. But the engine sounded clean, the heat blasted strong, and the price was about as good as she was going to get. It was just under four thousand after tax.

When the payment finally processed, Brielle stepped outside into the cold November air and looked at her new car. It wasn't what she wanted. It wasn't even close. But it was hers, and she needed it right now. She unlocked the door and slid into the driver's seat. The interior smelled faintly of old leather and cheap air freshener. She rested her hands on the steering wheel, exhaling. She leaned her head back and closed her eyes for a moment, letting the weight of everything settle. It wasn't the life she planned, not even close, but it was the one she was given, and she knew she had to make the most of it. She pulled out the lot and headed home.

THE MOMENT BRIELLE stepped back into the house, her phone rang. She set her keys on the table and glanced down at the screen. Her heart tightened when she saw it was Taj. She wasn't ready to talk to anyone, but she didn't want to ignore him. She swiped to answer.

"Hello?"

"Hey." Taj's deep voice came through the phone. "I just wanted to check on you, make sure you're alright."

Brielle closed her eyes for half a second. She didn't want him hearing the exhaustion in her voice or the emotions sitting right under her skin.

"Yeah," she said softly, forcing her voice to stay even. "I'm good."

It was a lie, and she knew it. But she didn't want pity from him or anyone else.

"You sure?" he pressed gently. "You don't really sound like you're okay. It sounded like a lot was going on yesterday. Just wanted to make sure you was straight."

"I am," she lied again. "Just tired, that's all."

Taj was quiet for a moment, as if he was scanning her words. "Alright," he finally spoke. "But listen... if you ever need anything, and I mean anything, you can just ask me. I'm serious, Brielle."

Her throat tightened unexpectedly at how genuine he sounded. She wasn't used to kindness these days, and she didn't know how to take it.

"Thank you, Taj. But I'm fine, really," she whispered.

"No problem. I'm just making sure," he replied. "I'll let you get some rest. Just... take care of yourself, okay?"

"I will. Thanks again, Taj. Have a good day."

"You too, Brielle."

The call ended, and Brielle lowered the phone, staring at the dark screen for a few seconds. She thought for a second about how comforting his voice felt. She sucked in a breath and pushed the thought aside. She kicked off her boots, leaving them by the door, before walking farther into the house. Her body felt heavy, tired in a way that sleep alone couldn't fix. She went to the kitchen, opened the fridge, and stared inside for a moment before shutting it again. She wasn't hungry. She wasn't anything except drained.

Walking into the living room, she turned on the TV for background noise and curled up on the couch, pulling a blanket over herself. The house felt colder than usual, maybe because she knew she wouldn't have it for long. Or maybe it was because everything familiar suddenly felt temporary.

Brielle scrolled through apartments on her phone for the next hour. Every place she found was either too high, too small, too far, or unavailable. She checked rent assistance programs, then job postings, along with maternity resources. All of it felt overwhelming. Eventually, she dropped the phone onto her chest and covered her eyes with her arm, letting the quiet fill the room.

After a while, she got up and made herself a bowl of cereal, Honey Nut Cheerios, the one thing she could stomach at the moment. She ate it on the couch, watching a show she wasn't paying attention to, her mind drifting from worry to exhaustion then back again. When the bowl was empty, she washed it, turned off the lights, and went to her bedroom. She changed into a big T-shirt and slid under the covers, placing a hand over her stomach, as she lay on her side.

"Please, God, let something work out in my favor and soon," she whispered into the darkness.

Chapter Nine

Over the next few weeks, Brielle tried everything she could to find a decent job but came up with nothing. Every morning, she woke up with a plan, résumé updates, online applications, walk-ins, cold calls. Yet every night, she went to bed with the same sinking feeling in her stomach. Now, she only had two weeks left in her house. Boxes sat flattened in the corner of her living room, untouched. She hadn't packed a single thing, more so because she couldn't. Every time she even thought about folding clothes or pulling dishes from the cabinet, her chest tightened and her throat burned. Packing made it real, and Brielle wasn't ready for real.

She didn't tell her mother or Amya what was going on. Every time she talked to them or saw them, she acted like everything was fine. Something deep in her kept insisting she needed to figure this out on her own, prove to herself she could. But as the days passed and the eviction deadline crept closer, that confidence turned into doubt. She didn't know where she was going to go. She didn't know what she was going to do. And late at night, lying awake in the dark with the silence pressing in too heavy, she was starting to think she wouldn't be able to do it alone after all.

Taj had been calling every couple of days, just to check in on her. Sometimes, it was a quick, "You good?" Other times, he tried to make small talk, asking if she'd eaten or if she needed anything.

She wasn't used to someone checking on her without wanting something in return. She wasn't used to a man's concern feeling genuine. Not after the games Delano had played with her. She didn't want to admit that his calls comforted her, but they did. Delano, on the other hand, hadn't reached out at all. Not a text or a call. It was like he'd fallen off the face of the earth, and part of her was relieved. The other part hurt more than she wanted to admit.

Ten days before she had to be out of the house, Brielle woke up with a sudden burst of energy, panic mixed with determination. She couldn't keep avoiding it. She knew she needed to start packing. She rolled out of bed, tied her hair up, and put on an old school R&B playlist. The music filled the house, bouncing off the walls and echoing through rooms that were about to belong to somebody else.

She grabbed the flattened boxes from the corner and got to work. The first one was the hardest, pulling books off the shelf, wrapping picture frames, folding clothes she hadn't worn in months. Every item made her heart thump a little heavier. But Brielle kept going. She still had no idea where she was going to go. She hadn't found a job. She hadn't saved enough. But she knew one thing, and that was her belongings would have to go into storage until she figured out the rest.

She spent the entire day packing, and by the time the sun set, she had packed mostly everything in her kitchen, bedroom, and bathroom, leaving out only the things she would need for the next couple of days. When she was done for the day, Brielle made herself a salad and watched TV on the couch for the rest of the night.

THE DAYS PASSED QUICKER than Brielle expected, and before she knew it, she was in her final week at the house. The walls felt smaller now, like they were pushing her into a corner she couldn't escape. The pressure of pretending, the weight of carrying everything alone, had gotten too heavy. She couldn't keep lying to the people who loved her. So, that evening, she called Denise and Amya over. They came with no hesitation, Amya full of energy the moment she walked through the door. They sat in Brielle's half-packed living room, boxes stacked along the wall, as Denise looked around the room, frowning.

"Aight," Denise spoke, dropping her purse on the couch. "What's going on? This don't look like no damn spring cleaning."

Brielle sat down across from them, her stomach tight. She took a breath before telling them everything. She told them how Delano had been lying to her the entire time. How he wasn't who she thought he was and how she was now being put out of her home because of it. She told them how she'd been trying to find a job with no luck and how she'd been keeping everything in, trying to handle it on her own. Her voice cracked on the last part. She wiped her eyes, embarrassed, but she kept going. She told them how scared she was to bring a child into all this and how she prayed she would have enough love to give to her child to make up for the dad not being around.

Denise was the first to react. She didn't even let Brielle finish before sliding into the empty spot beside her and pulling her into a tight hug.

"Baby, why didn't you tell me right away?" Denise's voice trembled with hurt. "You don't ever have to suffer by yourself. You hear me? You can always come home. Always. I don't care what the situation is. You will never be homeless. Not while I'm alive."

Brielle cried harder then, her face pressed against her mother's shoulder. All the strength she'd been forcing herself to hold onto crumbled. Amya was pacing, hands on her hips, jaw clenched.

"Nah, I'm pissed," she spoke. "For real. Delano foul than a muthafucka for this shit. That man got you stressed out like this, while you pregnant? Oh, he a different kind of ain't shit ass nigga. Just give me the word, sis. I'll have my cousin, Murk, go see 'bout that ass." She came over, kneeling in front of Brielle. "You should've told us sooner. You know we ride for you. Whatever you need, money, help packing, finding a job, gettin' that nigga's ass beat, I got you."

Both Denise and Amya wrapped Brielle in their arms, pulling her into a group hug. And for the first time in weeks, Brielle didn't feel like she was drowning. She felt safe, protected, and reassured. For the first time in weeks, the weight didn't feel so heavy because she now knew she wasn't carrying it alone.

After they left, the house felt different – still quiet, still cluttered with half-filled boxes, yet somehow lighter. Like some of the darkness she'd been holding had finally been pulled out of her chest. She now felt relieved and hopeful again. That night when Brielle went to bed, she was finally able to sleep peacefully.

OVER THE NEXT couple of days, Brielle had packed up her entire house with Amaya coming over every day to help her. Brielle rented a U-Haul, and Amya paid a few of her teenage cousins to move Brielle's things into her basement. Brielle had explained to Amya that she could put her items in storage, but Amya refused, telling Brielle that it was a waste of money when she had a basement that she didn't use. Brielle thanked her, and once all of Brielle's furniture was neatly placed in Amya's basement, Amya followed Brielle back to U-Haul to return the rental before heading to Denise's.

"You sure you don't want to stay with me? You know I got that extra bedroom and everything. It will be like an extended slumber party," Amya suggested the moment she pulled into Denise's driveway.

"That's sweet, but you need your space. It's bad enough I got my whole house in your basement. I can't be up in there too."

'Girl, please. You know fuck well it ain't shit for you to be there."

"Thank you, but this is something I gotta do for me. I have to learn this lesson so that I never have to go through this again."

Amya nodded her head, letting Brielle know she understood. They got out the car and retrieved Brielle's suitcases before going into the house. The house felt strange to her, not unfamiliar yet not where she wanted to be. Her old room was just as she'd left it the day she moved out. The fluffy pink comforter was tucked neatly into the bed, and she could tell that her mother had put fresh white sheets on it. The LED lights were set to pink, just like she always had them, and two champagne toast candles set on the nightstand next to her bed. Her dresser was still filled with the same old pictures that were always there. Her cheer trophies set on two floating shelves, and everything in the room reminded Brielle of who she used to be. However, this was not who she was anymore.

Brielle was now a grown woman, and most importantly, she was about to be someone's mother. Although she was thankful that she had somewhere to come to, she knew that she needed her own. There was no way that Brielle could bring a baby into the world without a home to call their own. So, it was at that moment that she knew she would do everything she could to ensure that she had her own place before the baby was born. Part of her felt like she'd failed by taking a step backward instead of forward. She hated that she needed help and hated the fact that she couldn't provide the stability she'd imagined when she had her first child. However, she knew she wouldn't stay down forever.

Amya stayed long enough to help Brielle put away her clothes before she left. Brielle had just sat on her bed when there was a soft knock on the door. Denise opened it a few seconds later, peeking her head in.

"I'm about to cook some dinner. How 'bout you come down to the kitchen and keep me company?"

"Okay, give me a second. I'm gonna take a quick shower and change clothes."

"Okay. I'm going to start cooking. Just come down when you done."

Brielle smiled, nodding her head, before Denise left, closing the door behind her. Just as promised, Brielle went right down to the kitchen after her shower. Denise was already at the stove, sautéing onions in a pan. There was chicken frying in a pan next to that, and everything to make macaroni and cheese sat on the counter.

"Dang, Ma, you got it smelling good up in here. What you cooking?"

"Yo' favorite meal. Fried chicken, potato salad, green beans, macaroni and cheese, and cornbread muffins," Denise replied with a smile.

"Now, Mama, you know you supposed to be eating healthy after that heart attack."

"This is healthy. This is soul food, baby, so this meal right here is going to nourish the soul. Ain't no pork in this shit either, so like I said, this is healthy."

Brielle shook her head, laughing off her mother's statement. She knew there was no way she was going to win this argument, so she thought it best to let it go – just for the night. Come tomorrow morning, Brielle was going to take it upon herself to bring healthier meal options and snacks into the house.

"You need me to help with anything, Mama?"

"Not really. This is your first night here, so I'm making this dinner for you. But if you want, you can make some Kool-Aid."

Brielle nodded, standing up from the table and walking over to the counter to grab the pitcher. "Grape or red?" she asked, looking over at her mother.

Denise thought for just a moment before replying. "Red."

When dinner was done, Denise made their plates, and they sat at the table to eat. Over dinner, Denise told Brielle that she could decorate her room any way she wanted. However, Brielle declined, letting Denise know that she didn't plan on being there long enough to decorate anything.

"You don't have to be in a rush to go anywhere. This is your home as much as it is mine. I understand you want your own but take your time. Save up some money so that you and the baby will be good when you finally do move out."

Brielle nodded her head slowly, knowing that what her mother was saying was true. The smart move would be for her to take this time and stack any money she could get. The problem was there was no money coming in. She knew that she wanted to have her own place by the time she had the baby. But until then, she was going to look for a job and save as much money as she could. When dinner was over, Brielle helped Denise clean the kitchen before they went into the living room and watched a movie.

By the time the movie was over, Brielle was exhausted. She hugged her mother good night before standing to her feet and going upstairs to her room. As she lay stretched out on her bed, staring up at the ceiling, she thought about the decisions that caused her to have to come back home. She'd loved and trusted a man that she now knew didn't love her back. She'd trusted him with everything, and he'd now taken it all away. Her hand rested on her stomach, thumb tracing slow circles through the fabric of her shirt.

She thought about how different her life looked from what she'd imagined just a few months ago. She was pregnant, newly single, and now starting over from her childhood home. For some, this may have been rock bottom. However, Brielle was going to use this as a crutch to get back on her feet and never find herself in this situation again.

Chapter Ten

A month had passed, and things had started looking up for Brielle. She'd managed to find a stay-at-home job scheduling appointments for a dentist's office. The pay wasn't great, barely enough to stack on top of what little savings she had left, but it was consistent. And right now, consistency mattered more than comfort. Every morning, she logged in from her childhood bedroom, headset on, computer on her desk, and a smile on her face. She had to remind herself that something was better than nothing. Her days followed a routine of answering calls and confirming appointments. By the end of each shift, she was exhausted yet grateful.

One afternoon, just before she was about to log off, her phone buzzed beside her keyboard, letting her know that she'd received a text message. Looking down at the phone, she saw it was from Amya.

> Amya: You got your doctor appointment tomorrow, right? You want me to come with you?

Brielle smiled softly at the screen. She typed back with one hand, the other resting on her stomach.

Her reply came almost instantly.

Brielle set her phone down and leaned back in her chair, exhaling slowly. Although Delano wasn't around, the support Brielle received didn't lack. If nothing else, she knew her mother and best friend had her back, and she loved that. As she shut down her computer for the day, a small smile tugged at her lips. She didn't have much figured out yet, but she knew she wasn't walking this journey alone, and that made the steps lighter.

The next morning, Brielle stood at her closet, trying to find something to wear. Late December had settled into the city, and the cold was bone chilling. Brielle had lived in Michigan her entire life, and this had to be the coldest winter she'd experienced. She was getting ready for her doctor's appointment. Dressing for comfort more than style, she slid into a pair of black maternity leggings that hugged her curves without squeezing, a soft oatmeal-colored sweater, and a long camel wool coat to keep the chill out. On her feet were tan UGG boots paired with thick socks. She'd switched out her blonde box braids for jet black ones, and they flowed long down her back. After she put on a pair of gold hoops and a swipe of lip gloss, she was ready to go.

She grabbed her purse and scarf, slipping it around her neck. Just as she reached for the doorknob, her phone rang. She glanced down at the screen and paused when she saw it was Taj. She answered the call, tucking the phone between her ear and shoulder, as she opened the door.

"Hey," she said softly.

"Hey. I was just checking on you," Taj replied. "I hadn't heard from you in a minute and wanted to make sure you were straight."

Brielle smiled to herself, as she made her way to her car. "Yeah,

I'm doing better. I moved in with my mom, so that helped a lot. And I got a new car. It's not much, but it gets me around. How are you?"

She started the car and sat back in her seat, as she waited for it to warm up.

"Oh, okay, look at you. That's what's up. I'm good, can't call it. Just tryna make it through the holidays. My nieces got me going crazy, looking for everything they put on these Christmas lists they sent me."

"Oh, you must be the rich uncle," Brielle joked.

"I'm the only one of my siblings that don't have any kids. My older sister has three girls, and my younger sister has one. And me, I'm just that uncle that gets them whatever they want."

"Aww, look at you. That's sweet. Are you at least almost done shopping?"

"Nope!" Taj laughed. "I haven't even started. I went out Saturday and couldn't find the first three things on my list. So, I went back home. I guess I gotta go back out if I plan to bring their gifts with me to Christmas dinner."

"Not you gave up. That's funny. You do know that sometimes you have to go to more than one store, don't you?"

"See, this is why I don't like shopping. I usually order everything online, but I waited too late this year. So now, I gotta go into the store."

"I love shopping, especially Christmas shopping," Brielle replied with a smile.

"Then how 'bout you go with me and keep me company?" Taj suggested.

"Okay, I'm on my way to my doctor's appointment right now. But I'm free tomorrow after five."

"Stop playing because I can be to pick you up by 5:01."

Brielle burst into laughter. "I'll be ready when you get here. I'll text you the address later today after my appointment."

"Okay, cool. Sounds like a plan to me.

They ended the call, and Brielle smiled, as she pulled out her mother's driveway, heading to her appointment.

BRIELLE SPOTTED Denise's car the moment she pulled into the parking lot. She had come straight from work. She must have just gotten there because she was still sitting in her car when Brielle parked next to her. Denise smiled at her before they both got out their cars and walked into the doctor's office together. Amya was already inside the waiting room, sitting in one of the chairs, scrolling through her phone.

"How did I know that you would already be here?" Brielle laughed, walking over to Amya.

Amya stood to her feet, and they hugged.

"About time y'all got here. How am I here before you, and it's your appointment?"

Brielle laughed before waking up to the desk to sign in. Brielle had been waiting on this very appointment since the day she found out she was pregnant. Today was the day she found out what she was having, and she couldn't have been more excited. She couldn't wait to start shopping for her child but wanted to wait to find out the gender before she did anything.

When the nurse finally called Brielle's name, excitement buzzed through her chest. The three of them stood at the same time and followed the nurse down the hallway, smiles plastered on all their faces. Inside the exam room, Brielle climbed onto the table, her heart racing. The lights dimmed, as the technician prepared the machine. Brielle watched in anticipation, as the technician squeezed gel onto her stomach. Brielle smiled, eyes darting from Denise to Amya. The screen flickered to life, and Brielle's heard raced.

"There we go," the technician spoke, adjusting the image. "Let's take a look."

Brielle held her breath, eyes glued to the monitor. The room felt quiet, like the air itself was waiting.

"Well," the technician uttered with a smile, pointing at the screen, "looks like you're having a healthy baby boy."

For a second, Brielle didn't move, then it hit her. "A boy?" she whispered.

Denise gasped, covering her mouth, as tears instantly filled her eyes. "My grandson," she murmured softly.

Amya squealed. "I knew it! I knew it was a boy!"

Brielle laughed through tears she didn't realize were falling, her hand instinctively moving to her stomach. She was having a boy. A little person was growing inside her, and she knew that she would do anything and everything to make sure he had the best life possible. In that moment, the fear of the unknown faded into the background, and all she felt was love

<hr>

AFTER THE APPOINTMENT, the three women stepped out into the cool December air, their spirits noticeably lighter. Denise couldn't stop smiling, pride and joy shining in her eyes. Amya kept repeating how a little man was finally on the way.

"I'm starving," Amya announced once they reached the parking lot. "And I want seafood. I want shrimp, potatoes, corn, crab legs. Hell, I want a whole damn boil."

Brielle laughed, as she pulled her eyes from her purse. "Well, Lily's is not too far from here. I've never been, but I heard it was good."

"They are good. And not crazy expensive," Denise added with a smile.

"Cool, then let's go," Amya spoke.

The three of them got into their cars, pulling out of the parking lot and heading to the restaurant. Inside, they were greeted by warm chatter and the smell of good seafood. They were seated quickly, and within minutes, the waitress was taking their drink orders. They looked over the menu before deciding what they were going to order.

"I'm getting the crab cake sandwich with a side of crab legs. What y'all getting?" Amya asked, looking over at Brielle and Denise.

Denise answered first. "I'm gonna get this fried fish plate."

"This salmon salad looks good. I think I'ma go with that," Brielle replied.

They laughed, talked, and ate good food, as they enjoyed each other's company. Brielle was happy that things were finally looking up for her. And she knew that it would only get better from here on out.

THE NEXT MORNING, Brielle got out of bed and went straight to the bathroom. Denise had already left for work, so the house was quiet. Once she'd taken her shower and brushed her teeth, she went back into her room wrapped in a towel. She put on a gray cotton two-piece set and wrapped her braids into a bun. She slipped her feet into her slippers and sat at her desk before putting on her headset and powering up her laptop. She spent her workday taking calls and making appointments. By the time 5:00 p.m. rolled around, she was more than ready to shut down her laptop and leave her desk.

She walked into the bathroom to freshen up, knowing that Taj would be there at any moment. When she was done, she walked back into her bedroom just as her phone rang. She answered it, seeing that it was Taj.

"I'm outside," he spoke the moment she answered.

"I'm coming now," she replied, a smile tugging at her lips.

She grabbed her purse and slid into her coat before walking out the door. Taj was waiting in his Range Rover, already leaned back casually in the driver's seat. He smiled when she climbed in, greeting her before pulling out the driveway.

"I hope you ready for all this damn shopping because I'm not," Taj joked.

"Oh, I was born ready. I don't think you understand how much I love Christmas shopping. It's so much fun."

"Well, that makes one of us."

Brielle laughed. "You said you had four nieces, right?"

"Yep, four little divas."

"How old are they?" Brielle inquired.

"So, my older sister had three. They're nine, seven, and two. Then, my younger sister has a five-year-old. And they all spoiled. Hence the full list they all gave me. And I know the two-year-old didn't write all this shit out, so I know her sisters had something to do with this."

She laughed. "I'm sure the list isn't that bad."

"Shit, wait til you see it. It's over fifty things on it between the four of them, and I'm only the uncle. I can only imagine what the list they gave to their parents looked like. I just really hope I can knock it all out in one trip. I don't want to do anymore shopping after today."

"I hear you. We gon' try to make that happen."

When they pulled into the mall parking lot, Brielle turned toward him. "Let me see the list."

Taj grabbed his phone and scrolled for a few before handing the phone to her. The list was long, just as Taj had told her it was. Each item had a name on the side to let Taj know who the gift was for. Brielle scanned the list before speaking again.

"Okay," she spoke, handing the phone back to him. "We need to start with the big stuff first then work our way down the list."

Taj smiled, impressed. "I knew bringing you was a good idea."

She smiled back, already mentally mapping out their shopping strategy, as they stepped out of the truck and into the mall, heading into the first store. They walked through the mall side by side, bags slowly accumulating in Taj's hands, as the list got shorter. Brielle moved with purpose, stopping in front of store windows, pointing things out, asking questions about each niece like she was really trying to get to know them. Christmas music played softly overhead, mixed with the sound of shoppers talking in the distance.

Brielle smiled, as she helped Taj pick out clothes for each niece. Two hours later, they stood near the mall exit surrounded by bags, both of them tired but satisfied. Taj shifted the weight in his arms and let out a low chuckle.

"I don't think I've ever been this successful in one trip," he admitted.

Brielle grinned. "See? You just needed the right help. Now, we just need to hit up a Walmart and get what's left on the list, along with wrapping paper, bows, and tape."

"Wrappin' paper? What I need that for?" Taj asked, turning to look at Brielle.

"To wrap the gifts."

"I never said I was wrapping anything. It's bad enough they sent me this long ass list. Now, I gotta wrap them too? Why can't they get this shit in the boxes and bags they came in?"

"Boy, you are not gonna do them babies like that. Part of getting a gift is the element of surprise. You not gon' take that away from them. You gonna wrap these gifts. And each one of the girls are going to get a different wrapping paper."

"What? Now you milking it." Taj laughed. "Come on so we can get to Walmart."

Brielle laughed, as they made their way to the car. Taj put everything in the truck before opening Brielle's door. She smiled, getting into the car, before leaning over and opening his door for him before they pulled off into the darkness.

WALMART WAS EXACTLY what Brielle expected it to be, full of people. Everyone was there trying to get their last bit of holiday shopping done. Taj grabbed a cart as soon as they walked in, and they made their way to the toy section.

"This is where shit gets real," Taj joked.

Brielle smiled. "You ain't lying. Kids get real serious about they toys."

They started with the youngest first. They thought she would be the easiest with her being only two. Brielle picked out a chunky plastic activity set with bright colors, buttons that lit up, and music that promised to be annoying in the best way. She added a plush teddy bear wearing a tiny holiday sweater, squeezing it once before dropping it into the cart. She grabbed a few other things for her as well, placing them into the cart with a smile. For the five, seven, and nine year olds, they stuck to the list that they had, grabbing several doll sets with all the accessories, two scooters, one pink and the other purple, several board games, a tea set, and kitchen set with all the food for them to cook.

They moved through the store easily, picking up everything they needed, until there was finally only one thing left on the list – a karaoke machine that Taj's oldest niece wanted. They moved on to the electronics, Taj finding the machine almost instantly. With the Christmas list officially complete, they turned down another aisle to walk up to the register, when Brielle came across the baby section. Brielle's heart warmed when she saw all the cute little baby clothes.

She reached for a soft gray onesie, simple yet sweet, and placed it into the cart. She added a pack of newborn socks and a set of pacifiers shaped like little stars. She pushed the cart slowly, Taj at her side, as she looked over items that caught her eye. She picked up two blankets, one blue and white and the other gray, and placed them into the cart as well.

"Okay, I'm done. I just wanted to get a few things to start with," Brielle spoke softly, looking up at Taj.

He smiled back at her. "I'm chillin'. You walked through the stores with me, getting everything I need, so go ahead and take as much time as you want."

"I'm done, really. I just wanted to get a few things because I don't have anything. I'm going to save the big shopping for closer to my due date. I plan to move before I have my baby, and I don't want to have to pack up any more than I already have to."

"Yeah, I feel you on that. What area do you want to live in?" Taj asked, as he took the overflowing cart from Brielle and pushed it toward the checkout area.

"It really doesn't matter seeing how I work from home. I just want something that's affordable and in a nice neighborhood."

"I feel you on that. Safety is most definitely important," Taj replied.

Taj rolled the cart to the register and piled the items on the belt. When the cart was empty, Brielle realized that Taj had not separated their items. She started taking her items off the belt and placing them in the back.

"What you doing that for? I was going to ask her to bag the baby stuff separately."

"I need to pay for them, Taj." Brielle chuckled, as she continued grabbing up her items.

"We might as well add it all together. I got it," he spoke, already pulling out his wallet.

Brielle frowned. "Taj, you don't have to pay for my stuff."

He looked down at her, a small smile tugging at his face. "I didn't say I had to. I want to. Let's just say it's part of a thank you for everything you did for me today."

She hesitated for just a moment then nodded her head. Taj gathered all the bags, placing them into the cart, before they walked out of the store. Once everything was packed neatly into the truck, Brielle climbed back into Taj's Range Rover, rubbing her hands together to warm them, as Taj started the engine.

He glanced over at her. "You hungry?"

Brielle blinked, surprised. She hadn't even realized how long it had been since lunch. It was nine-thirty at night, and Brielle hadn't eaten anything since two. Her stomach answered for her with a soft growl, and she laughed quietly. "Yeah, I actually am."

Taj smiled. "Good. Let me take you to get something to eat."

She hesitated for half a second then nodded. "Okay."

They drove through the city, Christmas lights blurring past the windows, the radio low in the background. Brielle rested back in her seat, watching the familiar streets go by, feeling relaxed, as she just enjoyed the ride. Taj pulled up to Andiamo's Steakhouse about ten minutes later.

"This okay with you?" he asked.

Brielle smiled. "Yeah. This is perfect."

Inside, the restaurant was calm and intimate. They were seated near the windows, giving them a beautiful view of the city lights. Brielle took off her coat and settled into her chair, smoothing her sweater over her stomach. Taj watched her for a moment before taking his seat across from her. They placed their orders, both wanting the same thing – filets cooked medium, mashed potatoes to share, and sautéed vegetables. Brielle opted for water with lemon, while Taj ordered himself a drink. They talked, while they waited on their food. Brielle still trying to convince Taj to use the wrapping paper they bought.

"I'll wrap them up if you come keep me company while I do it," he suggested.

The waitress was back at their table with their food before she could answer. She began putting mashed potatoes and vegetables on the plate with her steak. She stopped when she realized that Taj was staring at her.

"What?" She chuckled, looking up at him.

"I'm tryna see is you coming over to wrap gifts with me."

"You serious, huh? You really not gonna wrap your nieces' gifts unless I come keep you company?"

"I'll put a bow on that shit and call it a day."

"Fine, I'll come over tomorrow after work. I get off early tomorrow, so I should be to you by two if that's okay. You just gotta send me your address."

Taj wiped his hands on a napkin before pulling out his phone. Brielle's phone chimed a few seconds later, alerting her that she had received a text.

"There you go. I'll be home all day tomorrow, so just come when you're ready."

Brielle nodded her head, and the two of them enjoyed their meal together. They continued the conversation, and for the first time in months, Brielle felt content. Taj was like a breath of fresh air, and Brielle welcomed his friendship. When their plates were cleared and the check was taken care of, they left they restaurant.

When Brielle got back home that night, she was all smiles. Denise was in the living room, stretched out on the couch, the evening news playing softly, as images flashed across the screen. She glanced up when the front door opened, her eyes immediately landing on the shopping bags hanging from Brielle's arms.

"Well, look at you," Denise said, amused. "Where you been?"

Brielle slipped out of her coat and set the bags down by the door. "I was hanging with a friend," she replied casually, though the smile on her face refused to fade.

Denise raised an eyebrow but didn't push. Instead, she nodded toward the bags. "What you got there?"

Brielle's smile softened, as she reached inside one of them. "I picked up a few things for the baby."

She carried the bags into the living room and sat on the sofa, pulling the items out one by one. Denise's face changed instantly. Her eyes softened, and she leaned forward, reaching out to touch the fabric.

"Oh, Brielle," she said quietly. "These are so cute."

"I know! I couldn't help myself when I saw them," Brielle admitted, laughing softly. "I walked past the baby section, and that was all she wrote."

Denise smiled wide, pride shining through. "You're already such a good mama."

The words settled deep in Brielle's chest. "Thank you, Mama. I learned from you."

After everything was put away, Brielle headed upstairs. She took a long shower, letting the warm water wash away the day. She'd had a good time with Taj, and it felt so natural. She enjoyed his company and was now eager to see him that following day. When she finally crawled into bed, her body relaxed against the mattress, exhaustion settling in gently. As she lay there in the quiet, a small smile lingered on her lips. It had been a good day, and for the first time in a long time, she drifted off to sleep feeling happy.

THE NEXT DAY, after clocking out of work for the day, Brielle dressed in a pair of black leather pants and a white turtleneck. She slipped into a thick pair of socks and a pair of black Timbs before grabbing her coat and walking out the door. She'd promised Taj that she would come help him wrap his nieces' Christmas gifts, and that was exactly what she was going to do. So, she took the twenty minute drive to the address Taj provided after putting it into her GPS.

When she pulled up to his house, she had to do a double take, checking the address to ensure it was correct. The mansion was enormous. Smooth stone and brick framed the front of the home, and the carefully manicured lawn stretched out on either side of the long, winding driveway. Elegant lanterns lined the path, leading up to the front porch. A set of tall, arched windows reflected the winter sunlight, revealing glimpses of the grand interior. The double front doors were polished mahogany, adorned with brass handles that gleamed in the afternoon light.

On one side, a neatly trimmed hedge ran along the property line, separating the estate from the neighboring homes, which were also just as impressive. The driveway led to a three-car garage with sleek doors that matched the modern aesthetic of the home. Brielle parked her car at the end of the driveway, her jaw dropping slightly, as she took in the property. Pulling her coat tighter around her, Brielle stepped out of her car, feeling a mix of awe and nerves. She couldn't wait to see what the inside looked like. Taj must have seen her when she parked because he opened the door for her the moment she walked up to it. She smiled, stepping into the house.

"Hey," Taj greeted, his eyes lighting up at the sight of her.

"Hey to you too," she replied.

As he stepped aside to let her in, Brielle hesitated at the threshold, her eyes widening at the breathtaking interior. Polished marble floors gleamed under the soft glow of crystal chandeliers, and the walls were adorned with tasteful art in gold and black frames. A grand staircase curved elegantly to the second floor, its railing a dark wood that was polished to perfection. Taj walked beside her, guiding her through the house. Every detail seemed carefully curated with rich, warm tones, plush furniture, and subtle accents that gave the home a sense of both opulence and comfort.

Finally, they reached the living room. Brielle's eyes landed on the centerpiece, a towering Christmas tree, its branches perfectly fluffed and decorated with twinkling lights and elegant ornaments. Beneath it, neatly arranged, were stacks of gifts, stacked in neat piles and ready to be wrapped. A large, soft sectional sat in the middle, surrounded by low tables. A thick area rug in cream and gold anchored the space, and velvet throw pillows added color. Against one wall, a fireplace burned softly, the mantle decorated with garlands, candles, and holiday figurines. Floor-to-ceiling windows along the far wall overlooked the snow-dusted backyard, and elegant drapes framed the view, completing the scene of luxury.

Brielle's breath caught. "Wow," she whispered. "Your home is beautiful."

Taj smiled, a little amused at her reaction. "Come on, I want to show you the rest before we start wrapping," he said, leading her farther into the house.

Once they were done, they made their way back to the living room, settling on the floor. Taj used the remote to turn on Christmas music that played through the hidden speakers. He handed Brielle a pair of scissors and a roll of tape, and they began wrapping gifts, as they sang along to the music.

Halfway through, Taj paused and looked over at Brielle. "You hungry?"

Brielle nodded. "Yeah, a little."

"Alright," he spoke, pulling out his phone. "What do you want me to pull up on DoorDash?"

Brielle smiled, already knowing what she wanted. "I can go for a Detroit-style pizza. How 'bout Buddy's?"

Taj grinned and tapped a few buttons on his phone, placing the order. The Christmas music played softly in the background, as they continued wrapping gifts, laughing, and chatting, the warm glow of the tree reflecting off the neatly stacked presents. When the DoorDash delivery arrived, they set the gifts aside and dug in, slices of thick, cheesy pizza in hand. Between bites, they laughed and shared memories of childhood Christmases. Hours passed, and eventually, every gift was wrapped, labeled, and placed neatly under the tree. Brielle leaned back against the couch, stretching her arms, while Taj admired their work with a satisfied grin.

"Looks like we did good," he uttered.

"We sure did," Brielle replied, her eyes sparkling. "Your nieces are going to be really happy."

"Yeah, they are. And that's really all that matters."

"I'm going to get out of here. I got a long day tomorrow with it being Christmas Eve and all. But I need to use the bathroom first."

Taj nodded, and Brielle walked out the room and headed to the bathroom. When she was done, she walked back to the living room and gathered her things. Taj, being the gentlemen that he was, walked her out to her car. The cold air nipped at their cheeks, but neither seemed to mind. He wrapped his arms around her in a gentle hug, holding her for a moment longer than usual.

"Thank you for helping me tonight. I actually had fun wrapping gifts, and I know that was all because of you."

"You're welcome. I had a good time too," Brielle replied, smiling, as she unlocked her car.

She got in the car, Taj closing her door for her. She started her car, smiling, as she waved goodbye to Taj, as she backed out the driveway. She smiled all the way home, thinking about the warm feeling Taj gave her inside.

Chapter Eleven

The holidays came and went, and through it all, Brielle was still saving her money. She was now six months pregnant and had saved up a nice bit of money. One Saturday afternoon while she laid in bed, she decided to scroll through Zillow and set up a few house tours. Although she only needed two bedrooms, she wanted a three-bedroom house so that she could turn one of the bedrooms into her home office. She scrolled through several houses and found three that she really liked before setting up appointments to see one.

Over the past couple of months, Brielle had also started spending a lot of time with Taj, and although she didn't want to take their relationship to the next level while she was pregnant, she couldn't deny how much she liked him. He'd come into her life in what she thought was one of her darkest times and had shined his light on her. She'd just placed her phone back on her nightstand when it chimed, letting Brielle know she had a notification. Looking at her phone, she saw it was an email. The property owner for one of the houses had emailed her back, letting Brielle know that he was open to show the house at three that day.

She quickly emailed back, letting him know that she would be there, before getting out of bed and heading into the bathroom to get herself together. She'd just gotten out the shower and walked back into her room when her phone began to ring. She pulled the towel tighter around her body, as she picked her phone up from the nightstand. Brielle smiled when she saw it was Taj.

"Hey, what you up to on this sunny afternoon?" Brielle answered.

"Don't let the sunshine fool you. It's cold as hell out there. But I'm not up to anything. I was callin' to see what you had up for the day."

"Well, right now, I'm about to get dressed so that I can go see this house. I found it on Zillow, and the owner emailed me back, telling me I could see it today at three."

"Oh, word? That's what's up. You want me to roll with you?"

"Yeah, I wouldn't mind the company." Brielle smiled.

"Cool, maybe we can go get some lunch after."

"You know I'm always down to eat, so that sounds like a plan."

"Cool, let me get dressed, and I'll be there about two-fifteen," Taj replied before ending the call.

When Brielle's phone rang at exactly two-fifteen, she knew it was Taj telling her he was outside. She smiled, answering and letting him know she'd be right out. After putting on some lip gloss, Brielle grabbed her purse and coat and walked out the door. She smiled, greeting him, as she got into the car.

About fifteen minutes later, they pulled up to the address of the house she'd found on Zillow, the neighborhood immediately making them both frown. The houses on either side were worn, some with peeling paint and boarded-up windows. Trash littered a few yards, and the faint sound of barking dogs echoed in the distance.

"You sure you want to go see this house?" Taj asked, looking over at Brielle.

She looked over at the house then back at Taj. "Yes, I want to see it. The pictures of the inside were beautiful."

"I can't imagine this house looking any better on the inside than it does on the outside. But if you insist, then come on."

The exterior paint on the house was faded, and the bricks

were chipped in several places. The lawn was patchy, mostly dirt with a few stubborn weeds poking through. The front door sagged slightly on its hinges, and the mailbox leaned at a sharp angle. Brielle frowned before they even got out of the car, hoping that the inside did the house some justice. They walked up the steps slowly and knocked on the door. When it opened, Taj stepped in first then Brielle after. A short, bald man stood on the other side.

"Hi there! You must be Brielle," he spoke warmly. "I'm Marcus. Come on in and I'll show you the place."

As she stepped farther into the house, Brielle was momentarily distracted by the faint smell of cleaning supplies mixed with something musty. The living room was small and cramped, the walls painted a dull beige that had seen better days. The carpet had stains in random spots, and she wondered if that was where the odor was coming from. The kitchen was tiny as well with scratched countertops and old wooden cabinets, and although the house came with the appliances, they were all white. A small window let in some light, but it couldn't compete with the dingy feel of the room. The bedrooms were even worse, barely enough space for a crib in the smaller one, and the closet doors were off their tracks.

Brielle's stomach sank. She moved slowly from room to room, her hands gripping her purse strap. She couldn't imagine raising her child in a place like this. It felt unsafe, uninviting, and far from the warm, stable home she wanted to provide for her child. Taj noticed her hesitation and gave her hand a gentle squeeze.

"It's okay," he said softly. "We'll keep looking."

Brielle nodded, forcing a small smile, because she knew this house was nowhere near what she needed. She had hoped, just for a moment, that it could work, but reality had quickly shattered that idea. They climbed into Taj's Range Rover, the engine humming to life, as they pulled away from the sketchy neighborhood.

"I still can't believe that place," Brielle uttered, shaking her head. "It looked nothing like the pictures online."

Taj chuckled softly. "Yeah, real estate photos can be deceiving. Don't worry though. I know someone in real estate. I'll see if they have any houses available that are actually worth looking at. He actually owes me a few favors."

Brielle smiled, grateful. "Thank you, Taj. I really appreciate that."

"No problem," he replied, glancing at her. "So, where do you want to go to eat? You've earned a little comfort after that disaster of a house tour."

Brielle's eyes lit up immediately. "Texas Roadhouse. I need their bread and cinnamon butter asap."

Taj laughed. "Alright, sounds like a plan. Let's get you fed."

When they arrived at Texas Roadhouse, Taj opened the door for Brielle, giving her a charming smile. She stepped inside, immediately feeling the comforting warmth of the restaurant and the familiar smell of freshly baked bread. They were seated right away at a booth near the window, and Brielle was starting to feel better already. The waitress approached with a pen and notepad, ready to take their orders. Before she could speak, Brielle and Taj exchanged a quick glance.

"Steak," Brielle said confidently, smiling. "With a loaded baked potato and broccoli."

"I'll have the same," Taj added.

The waitress raised an eyebrow but nodded, scribbling down their order before walking away. As they waited for their meals, Brielle and Taj couldn't help but laugh again about the house they had just seen.

"I still can't believe they thought anyone would want to live there," Brielle uttered between bites of bread, smearing a generous amount of cinnamon butter across her roll.

Taj chuckled, shaking his head. "I mean... some people really must think pictures can work magic. But that? Definitely not."

Their laughter bounced off the walls, filling the booth with warmth and easing the stress of the day. When the steaks arrived, perfectly cooked and steaming, they continued to joke, savoring both the food and the easy comfort of each other's company.

After they finished eating and the bill was paid, Brielle and Taj got up to leave. As they approached the door, Taj paused and looked at her.

"Hold on. I have to hit the bathroom real quick," he revealed, handing her his key fob. "You can wait in the car if you want."

Brielle nodded, clutching the fob inside her hand. She watched as Taj disappeared into the bathroom, the door swinging softly behind him. For a few seconds, she hesitated, unsure whether to wait or step outside. Finally, she decided she would go to the car. She reached for the door handle, pushing it open, and in the next moment, chaos struck. A teenage boy came barreling through the door at full speed, completely unaware of her presence. He collided with her stomach with a force that knocked her off balance, sending her sprawling backward onto the pavement.

Pain shot through her midsection, and she gasped, hands instinctively clutching herself. Shocked and disoriented, she tried to push herself up, the cold air stinging her skin and the world tilting around her. People around them gasped and murmured, as the boy skidded past, barely noticing the mess he'd caused. Brielle's heart raced, as she steadied herself, looking down at her stomach and feeling a surge of fear and panic. Tears pricked her eyes, both from the pain and the terror.

"Brielle!" Taj called, skidding to a stop beside her. "What happened? Are you okay?"

She could barely speak, shaking her head, fear still gripping her. Taj crouched beside her, hands gentle but firm, checking her over, his eyes darting to her stomach.

"I... I don't know," she finally stammered, her voice trembling. "It... it hurts."

Taj's jaw tightened, his protective instincts kicking in. "We're getting you checked, right now," he said, picking her up and carrying her to his truck.

Every step felt heavy with dread, but Brielle clung to the hope that her baby was okay. Taj didn't think; he just moved, putting Brielle into the truck and running around to the driver's seat. His tires squealed, as he hit the street, his hands gripping the steering wheel, eyes locked on the road. He ran red lights without hesitation, horn blaring, as cars swerved out of his way. At one point, he hopped a curb just to avoid traffic, muttering curses under his breath.

"Just breathe, Bri," he coached, voice tight but steady. "We almost there."

She sat, curled slightly in the seat, arms wrapped protectively around her stomach, fear pooling heavy in her chest. She nodded, even though tears blurred her vision. She could feel the adrenaline pumping through him as he drove. She closed her eyes and said a silent prayer that everything was okay. When the hospital finally came into view, Taj didn't bother looking for parking. He pulled straight up to the front entrance, throwing the truck into park before it fully stopped. He jumped out, ran to the other side, and yanked open Brielle's door.

"I got you," he spoke.

Before she could say another word, he scooped her up into his arms, holding her close like she weighed nothing. Brielle gasped softly, clutching his jacket, as he rushed inside the moment the automatic doors opened.

"Help!" Taj barked the moment his boots hit the floor. "She's pregnant. She fell on her stomach."

Nurses immediately rushed toward them, calling out instructions. One of them grabbed a wheelchair, and Taj gently lowered Brielle into it. However, he didn't leave her side. He stayed right there, towering protectively over her, as they rolled her down the hall.

Bright lights flooded the room, as nurses moved with urgency, their voices calm but quick. Electrodes were placed on her stomach, a blood pressure cuff tightened around her arm, and a monitor began to beep steadily beside her. Brielle lay back on the bed, hands trembling, as she stared up at the ceiling, every sound amplifying her fear.

"Please... please make sure my baby's okay," Brielle spoke out loud.

Taj stood near the foot of the bed, his jaw clenched so tight it ached. He watched every movement they made, every machine they hooked her to. When she reached out for him, he stepped closer immediately.

"Can you call my mom and my best friend?" Brielle asked, pointing over at her purse that sat on the chair. "My phone is in there, and the code is 0813. I need them to know what's going on."

Taj nodded, walking over to Brielle's purse and retrieving the phone. He stepped just outside the room, scrolling until he found the contact labeled *Mommy*. His chest felt heavy, as the line rang.

"Hey, baby girl. What's up?" Denise answered.

"Hello, this is Taj, and I'm a friend of Brielle," he spoke, keeping his voice steady. "I'm with Brielle right now. She was involved in an accident, and we're at Harper Hospital."

Silence stretched for half a second too long. "An accident? Is my baby okay?" Denise asked, panic creeping into her voice.

"She's awake and alert," Taj assured her. "They're running tests now just to make sure the baby is okay. She asked me to call you."

"I'm on my way," Denise said immediately. "I'm leaving right now."

Taj hung up and found the contact that read *Bestie*. She answered on the second ring.

"Hey, girl, I was just thinking about you. Do you..."

"This isn't Brielle," Taj cut in, urgency lacing his tone. "My name is Taj. I'm a friend of Brielle's. She had an accident, and we're at Harper Hospital."

"What?" Amya's voice jumped an octave. "Is she okay? Is the baby okay?"

"They're checking now," he replied. "She wanted me to call you."

"I'm already grabbing my keys," Amya answered. "Tell her I'm coming."

Taj returned to the room just as a nurse adjusted the monitor. Brielle's eyes found him instantly.

"They're on the way," he said softly. "Both of them."

Relief flickered across her face, though the fear never fully left. She nodded, swallowing hard, as the doctor explained the next steps, mentioning ultrasounds and observation. Brielle listened, but her focus stayed locked on the steady beeping beside her, each sound a reminder of what was at stake. Less than fifteen minutes later, Denise rushed into the room, eyes wild with worry. Amya wasn't far behind her.

"Oh, my God," Denise whispered, moving straight to Brielle's side and gently touching her face. "Are you okay, baby girl?"

"I'm okay, Mama," Brielle replied softly, though her voice cracked. "They're checking on him now."

Amya leaned over the bed next, her usual humor nowhere to be found. "You scared the hell outta me. You can't be doing that shit," she uttered.

Brielle managed a weak smile. "It scared me. It all happened so fast."

Denise took Brielle's hand, holding it tight, while Amya stood on the other side, rubbing her arm comfortingly. Taj remained close, just behind them, watching the two women gather around Brielle like a shield, worry written all over their faces. He tried to stay out of the way, tried to give Brielle space with her mother and best friend, but his eyes never left her.

About thirty minutes later, a nurse returned and let them know it was time for Brielle's ultrasound. Denise kissed Brielle's forehead before stepping back, whispering a quick prayer under her breath. Amya squeezed Brielle's hand.

"Everything gon' be fine, best friend," Amya spoke softly.

Brielle was wheeled out the room with her mother, Amya, and Taj left behind. The ultrasound room was dimly lit, the screen glowing faintly in the corner. Brielle's heart pounded, as the technician lifted her shirt and applied the cool gel to her stomach. She sucked in a breath, as her hands clenched at her sides. The technician worked quietly at first, eyes focused on the screen, moving the wand slowly. The silence felt unbearable. Brielle's chest tightened, tears threatening to spill, as she searched the technician's face, trying to read it. Then the sound of a steady rhythmic heartbeat filled the room. Brielle gasped softly, her breath hitching, as relief crashed into her so hard it almost hurt.

"That heartbeat is strong," the technician voiced, offering Brielle a reassuring smile. "Very strong."

Brielle nodded, tears slipping down the sides of her face, as she stared at the screen, overwhelmed with emotion. Her baby was fine. Everything was going to be okay, and Brielle couldn't have been happier.

"I would say that your baby is just fine. But we have to wait on the doctor to confirm that," the technician continued.

She nodded her head slowly. "Okay."

When she was done, she was wheeled back into her room and got back into the bed. She told her mother, Amya, and Taj what the ultrasound tech had told her, and relief filled the room. They all waited together for the doctor to come in and tell them that everything was fine and that Brielle could go home.

Brielle lay back against the pillows, staring at the ceiling, her fingers absently tracing circles over her stomach. Every sound in the hallway made her heart jump. Denise sat close, whispering prayers under her breath, while Amya paced near the window. Taj hadn't moved from his spot beside the wall, his eyes fixed on Brielle like she might disappear if he looked away.

"What the hell is taking so long? If everything was okay, why is it taking this long for the doctor to come in and say that?" Brielle questioned, frustration evident in her tone.

"Relax, baby. They probably have a lot of patients here today. He'll be in soon," Denise assured.

Brielle nodded her head, taking a few deep breaths, as she tried to calm down. She'd heard the heartbeat herself and heard the tech say how strong it was. So, she knew her son was fine. She just needed the doctor to come in and confirm it. When the doctor finally walked in, the room went silent. He flipped through Brielle's chart then looked up at her with a calm, reassuring expression.

"Good news," he spoke. "Your baby is fine," he continued. "Heartbeat is strong, and there's no sign of trauma."

The tears ran down Brielle's cheeks before she could stop them. Relief washed over her so fast her body trembled. Denise covered her face, tears spilling through her fingers, while Amya let out a loud breath that she'd clearly been holding in.

"Oh, thank God," Denise whispered.

The doctor went on, his tone firm but gentle. "That being said, this was still a scare. For the rest of your pregnancy, you're going to need to take it easy. No strenuous work, no heavy lifting, and I want you to listen to your body. If something doesn't feel right, you come straight back in."

Brielle nodded quickly. "I will," she said, her voice still shaky. "I promise."

"We're going to keep you for observation a little longer, just to be safe," the doctor added. "But right now, everything looks good."

When he left the room, the tension finally broke. Denise leaned over and kissed Brielle's forehead. "I told you everything would be okay. My grandbaby is strong, just like his mama."

Amya wiped at her eyes, forcing a small smile. "Exactly! Little man already showing he's tough."

Brielle turned her head slightly, her gaze finding Taj. He met her eyes, and for the first time since the accident, the tightness in his face eased.

"Thank you for everything, Taj," she spoke quietly, emotion thick in her voice.

Taj stepped closer to the bed. "It's no need to thank me, I did what anyone else would have done."

Brielle nodded her head, thankful for Taj's quick reaction. As she laid back in the hospital bed, she was finally able to breathe, knowing her son was healthy.

After the doctor left, Brielle had told Taj that he could go and didn't have to spend the rest of his evening at the hospital with her. However, he stayed, telling her that he wasn't leaving until she did. Brielle smiled, looking around the room at all the love and support her and her unborn child had.

ABOUT TWO HOURS LATER, the doctor was back in the room, handing Brielle her discharge papers. He stood at the foot of the bed, going over her instructions one last time, his tone firm. "Strict bed rest," he emphasized. "That means minimal movement. No unnecessary walking. No stress if it can be avoided. If you feel pain, dizziness, or cramping, you come straight back."

Brielle nodded, taking it all in. "I understand."

Denise stood close, already in mother mode, mentally rearranging everything she needed to do to make sure her daughter didn't lift a finger. Amya hovered nearby, arms crossed, her face serious, as she watched Brielle. Once the doctor left and the nurse finished disconnecting the monitors, Brielle slowly slid off the bed, moving carefully. Taj stepped forward instinctively, ready to help, but paused when Denise placed a steadying hand on Brielle's arm.

Brielle looked at Taj with a smile. "I'm going to ride back with my mama," Brielle spoke softly. "I'll call you later."

Taj nodded, though disappointment flickered briefly across his face before he masked it. "That's cool," he replied. "Just take it easy. Please."

She gave him a small smile. "I will. And Taj... thank you for everything."

Before he could respond, Brielle stepped forward and wrapped her arms around him. The hug was gentle and full of gratitude. Taj hesitated for only a second before hugging her back, his hand resting lightly between her shoulder blades, protective without being possessive.

"Anytime. You don't have to thank me, Brielle."

They pulled apart, and for a moment, neither of them spoke. Their eyes locked, and it was almost as though they were seeing each other for the first time. Finally, Denise cleared her throat before breaking the silence.

"Alright, baby. Let's get you home."

They made their way out of the hospital together, the night

air colder than it was before she went inside the building. Brielle climbed carefully into her mother's car, as Amya told them that she was going to follow them home. Denise started the car, turning on her music, as she pulled out of the parking lot. As the hospital disappeared behind them, Brielle leaned her head back against the seat, exhaustion settling in. She placed a hand over her stomach, feeling a quiet sense of relief. Her baby was okay, and she was going to do everything in her power to ensure it stayed that way.

When they finally made it inside the house, Amya wasted no time grilling Brielle, questions pouring out the moment they stepped in the door.

"So, that fine ass man that was at the hospital with you today," Amya looked at Brielle with a raised eyebrow, "was that the same man from the accident? The one that waited in the waiting room for you until you were discharged?"

Brielle froze for half a second then sighed. "Yes. That was Taj."

"Okayyy," Amya dragged out, already grinning. "And how long have y'all been talking?"

Brielle slipped her shoes off slowly, suddenly very interested in lining them up by the door. "We kept in touch after the accident, but it's not like that. We're just friends."

"The way that man was towering over you protectively in that hospital didn't seem like y'all were just friends. The way he looked at you, I know that look anywhere. Friends don't look at friends like that. He didn't even want to leave your side. That man thinks of you as more than a friend, baby girl." Denise laughed. "That man cares about you and that baby too. Clearly."

"Let me find out he a good man, Savannah. And wanna be a step daddy to my nephew." Amya chuckled.

"Relax, it's not like that at all. He's just a good person, and we just friends. That's it." Brielle shrugged.

Denise stood up and walked closer, placing a gentle hand on Brielle's arm. "Whatever he is," she said calmly, "I can tell that he really cares about you. Way more than Delano's bitch ass."

"Speaking of him, have you talked to him at all?" Amya asked.

"Nope, not at all. He made his choice and clearly doesn't want to be in my child's life, and I'm not going to beg him to. If he don't want to be here, then we better off without him."

"I know that's right, baby girl. Women have been raising children alone for years before us. I'm not saying it's right. I'm just saying it can be done," Denise uttered.

"That's right, Mama D, let her know. That man ain't stopping shit!" Amya yelled.

Brielle laughed weakly, exhaustion written all over her face. "I'm tired, y'all. It's been a long day. I'm gonna take a shower and lay down."

"Okay, go get some rest, baby. Just call me if you need anything, and I'll bring it up to you," Denise said immediately. "Doctor said bed rest, and that's exactly what it's going to be."

Brielle nodded, saying good night to both her mother and best friend, before heading upstairs. She walked into her room, grabbed her robe, and walked into the bathroom where she took a long, hot shower. When she was done about an hour later, she made her way back into her room and oiled her body before climbing in bed and drifting off to sleep.

Chapter Twelve

It was Saturday afternoon, and Brielle had been on bed rest for the past two weeks. With Denise being at work, the house was silent. And for the first day since she'd left the hospital, Amya hadn't stopped by. Brielle lay stretched across her bed, pillows propped behind her back, as she flicked through Netflix, trying to find something to watch that she hadn't already seen. Her phone buzzed, and she glanced down at it to see that it was Taj.

"Hey," she answered cheerfully.

"Hey," Taj greeted, his voice warm. "You busy?"

She looked around her room. There were two books on her nightstand that she'd already read, along with several bags of half-eaten snacks. "Nope, I'm not busy at all. I'm actually bored just sitting here. My mama is at work, so I'm just sitting here all alone."

There was a brief pause on the other end before he spoke again. "You want some company?" he asked.

"Yeah," she replied honestly. "I do."

Taj chuckled softly. "Alright. I'll come by, if that's okay with you."

"Yes, come keep me company please." Brielle laughed.

They hung up, and Brielle set her phone down before slowly getting out of bed. She went to the bathroom to freshen up before heading back into her room and changing her clothes. When she was done, she headed downstairs and took a seat on the couch. About thirty minutes later, there was a knock at the door. When she opened the door, Taj stood there with a brown paper bag in his hand, the familiar smell of Chinese food instantly filling the air.

"Hope you're hungry," he said with a smile.

Brielle smiled back, warmth spreading through her chest. "I'm pregnant. I'm always hungry." Brielle laughed, as she stepped to the side.

"Great because I got Golden Bowl, and I'm starving."

"Make yourself comfortable," Brielle said, nodding toward the couch. "I'll be right back. I'm going to grab us some plates."

"Okay, cool."

Brielle walked into the kitchen, pulling plates from the cabinet and grabbing napkins and utensils. When she returned to the living room, Taj was already sitting on the couch, leaning back comfortably, his attention on her the moment she walked in.

"Alright," she said, setting the plates down. "Let's eat."

Brielle eased herself down carefully, pillows tucked behind her back and at her side, while Taj spread the containers of Chinese food across the coffee table. He opened containers of orange chicken, egg foo young, shrimp fried rice, lo mein, and crab rangoons.

"Damn, you got all this food just for the two of us?" Brielle asked, looking down at the spread.

"Didn't know what your go to Chinese order was. And I wanted to surprise you, so I thought it was best to get a few options."

She laughed softly. "Well, thank you. I love Chinese."

They filled their plates, settling back in, as Brielle grabbed the remote. She scrolled through the apps for a moment before opening up the Prime app. She scrolled through a few movies before finally settling on one.

"Have you seen *Love Jones*?" she asked, glancing at him.

Taj smirked. "Of course I've seen *Love Jones*. That's a classic."

"Okay, good," she replied, pressing play.

Brielle relaxed back onto the couch, plate balanced carefully on her lap. Taj stretched his long legs out in front of him, one arm resting along the back of the couch. They ate quietly at first, both caught in the familiarity of the movie. Every now and then, Brielle would recite a line from the movie, and Taj would laugh.

"See, this is where he messed up," Taj said midway through, pointing his fork at the screen. "You can't be emotionally unavailable and still want all the benefits."

Brielle glanced at him, surprised and a little impressed. "That's accurate."

He shrugged. "I got two sisters, so I know." He laughed.

She turned to him and nodded, her thoughts drifting briefly to Delano and all the things that she'd accepted that she shouldn't have. Here she was, pregnant with his child, and not only had he gotten her kicked out of her home, but he was nowhere to be found. She would be lying if she said that didn't bother her from time to time; however, she knew there was nothing she could do about it. He'd made up his mind, and if his choice was to leave, Brielle wouldn't hold on to him.

When the movie ended, Brielle wiped her hands on a napkin and took their plates into the kitchen, while Taj packed up the leftover food. When she walked back into the living room, she sat back on the couch and picked up the remote again. She handed it to Taj. "Your turn to pick something."

Taj grinned, taking the remote from her, before scrolling through the movies and landing on *Dead Presidents.*

Brielle gasped dramatically. "Oh, this my shit."

"Good," he said, pressing play. "Because it's mine too."

Without realizing it, she leaned slightly toward him, drawn in by his warmth. Taj didn't move away either. Instead, he shifted just enough to make her more comfortable. She laid her head on his shoulder, as they watched the movie. They fell into a comfortable silence, the movie filling the space between them. When *Dead Presidents* ended, Brielle reached for the remote again, ready to pick the next movie.

She landed on *Brown Sugar* next. Brielle curled her legs slightly under her, getting more comfortable. Taj noticed and adjusted the pillow beside her without saying a word, gently nudging it closer, so she had more support. She studied him for a moment and how carefully he moved with her. He was so calm and gentle that it seemed unfamiliar. It was the complete opposite of the chaos she'd seen from Delano.

"I'm glad you came over today." She smiled.

"Me too," he replied. "I'm having a great time spending time with you."

She smiled. "I'm having a great time too."

They sat, curled up on the couch, as they watched the movie. When it was over, neither of them moved. They stayed there, on the couch, cuddled against each other. Finally, Taj broke the silence.

"If you want, I can go, but it's leftover food in the bag. You can have it as a late night snack."

Brielle smiled, nodding at Taj. "Thanks, the kitchen is right through that door." She pointed.

She watched him gather the bag and disappear into the kitchen. When he returned, he sat back down, this time a little closer than before. The TV continued playing softly in the background, some random movie trailer neither of them paid attention to. Brielle shifted slightly, adjusting the pillow behind her back. Taj turned toward her at the same time, their eyes meeting, holding each other's gaze for a second too long. Neither of them spoke. Taj's gaze dropped briefly to her lips then back to her eyes, like he was asking without saying a word. Brielle's heart began to race, her breath shallow, as emotion swelled in her chest. She didn't pull away but instead leaned in.

The kiss was soft at first, tentative, like both of them were testing the ground beneath their feet. But the second their lips touched, something sparked, warm and electric. Taj's hand lifted instinctively, hovering at her cheek before resting there gently. Brielle melted into the kiss for just a moment, her fingers curling into the fabric of his shirt. Then, reality rushed in. *What the fuck am I doing? I'm pregnant by someone else. I can't be kissing him.*

Brielle pulled back, breath shaky, her eyes wide as if she'd just startled herself. "I'm sorry," she uttered quickly, sitting back. "I shouldn't have done that."

Taj froze, his hand dropping back to his lap immediately. "Brielle..."

"No," she said softly but firmly, shaking her head. "I shouldn't have kissed you. I'm not... I'm not in a position to be anything but your friend, and I know that." Brielle pointed down at her stomach. "I'm pregnant," she continued, her voice cracking just slightly, "and my life is already complicated. I don't want to lead you on or blur lines that shouldn't be blurred."

Taj studied her face for a long moment then nodded slowly. "I hear you. And I respect that," he said sincerely. "And I don't want anything to happen that you don't want to happen. Ever."

Her eyes softened. "Thank you for understanding."

"Always," he replied. "I should probably head out."

Brielle nodded, standing slowly. "Yeah, that's probably best."

They walked to the door together. Taj paused for a moment before opening it, giving her a small smile. "Get some rest, okay?"

"I will. Thanks," she replied.

He stepped outside, pulling the door closed behind him. Brielle stood there for a long moment after he left, her heart still fluttering, her mind replaying the kiss she wasn't sure she should regret. Then, she turned off the lights and headed back up to her room, knowing things had shifted between them.

***

Monday morning came quickly, and it was back to work as normal. Brielle lay propped up in bed with her laptop resting against her thighs, headset on, as she worked through appointment confirmations and scheduling calls. Even days after, her mind was still on Taj and their kiss. His lips were soft, while his touch was firm. She tried to focus on her work, but she couldn't get him off her mind. She hadn't heard from him since he'd left her house Saturday night, and even though she told herself she understood why, the silence still tugged at her chest.

She sighed softly, fingers moving across the keyboard, as she confirmed another appointment. *Maybe I overreacted,* she thought. *Maybe I pushed him away.* Almost as if he could hear her thoughts, her phone buzzed beside her. Her heart jumped when she glanced down and saw his name on the screen.

Taj: Call me on your break.

A small smile curved her lips, as she picked up her phone to text him back. The rest of her workday dragged, but when her break finally came, Brielle didn't hesitate. She grabbed her phone and called Taj.

"Hey," she greeted when he answered.

"Hey," Taj replied, his voice warm and familiar. "You good?"

"Yeah," she said honestly. "I am. How are you?"

"I'm good. I wanted to let you know that I talked to my homeboy, the one I told you about in real estate," Taj explained. "He got back with me about two houses he's got for rent."

Brielle sat up a little straighter. "Seriously?"

"Yeah," he said. "He sent me the info this morning. I told him about your situation, and he said you could do virtual tours for both places."

Her eyes filled with water instantly, happiness rushing through her so fast it caught her off guard. "Taj... thank you so much. You have no idea what that means to me."

"You're welcome," he said simply. "I'm gonna send you the links. You can check them out when you get off work, and we can get the ball rollin'."

"I will," she replied, her voice thick with gratitude. "Thank you, Taj."

"No problem. Call me after you look at them and we'll go from there."

She nodded, smiling so hard her cheeks hurt. "I will."

They hung up shortly after, and Brielle set her phone down, pressing her hand lightly over her stomach, as she exhaled. Things were looking up, and Brielle couldn't have been more excited. She smiled through the rest of her workday, as she answered calls and made appointments.

When Brielle finally clocked out for the day, she didn't even bother leaving her bed. She shut her laptop, slid it to the side, and reached for her phone. She opened the first link Taj had sent her, her heart thudding, as the virtual tour loaded. The screen shifted to an exterior shot first. The house was a two-story brick colonial, sitting back from the street with a long concrete driveway and a detached two-car garage in the back. The brick was a deep reddish-brown, clean and well-maintained, with white trim framing the windows. A small, covered porch stretched across the front, wide enough for a small table and a couple of chairs. The front lawn was neatly cut, bordered by low hedges, and a young maple tree stood off to the side. Brielle tilted her head.

"This is nice," she murmured to herself.

Clicking forward, she moved inside the home. The front door opened into a formal living room, spacious and bright. Hardwood floors ran throughout the entire first level, polished and warm-toned. Sunlight poured in through large front windows, bouncing off cream-colored walls and white crown molding. She clicked again and entered the next room.

A formal dining room sat just beyond the living room, separated by a wide archway. There was a modern chandelier hanging low over the center of the room and enough space for a six or eight-seat table. Brielle imagined herself hosting parties and holiday dinners there. Then, she clicked again and moved on to the kitchen. It was fully updated with granite countertops, stainless steel appliances, and white cabinetry with brushed nickel handles. A small island sat in the center, perfect for prepping meals. It was beautiful, clean, and almost too perfect.

The tour continued into a half-bath on the first floor then into a family room at the back of the house. A fireplace was built into one wall, flanked by tall windows that overlooked the backyard. The space was large enough for a sectional couch, a media setup, maybe even a play area. She clicked again, and this time was on the second level of the house where there were three bedrooms.

The primary bedroom was massive, with high ceilings and an en-suite bathroom that featured double sinks, a soaking tub, and a walk-in shower. The walk-in closet was almost a room by itself, and Brielle imagined hanging her clothes inside. The second and third bedrooms were smaller but still decent-sized, each with good closet space and big windows. The tour ended in the backyard, which was fenced in and spacious though mostly empty.

Brielle leaned back against her pillows, letting out a slow breath. House one was beautiful. There was no doubt in her mind about that. However, with it just being her and the baby, she wasn't sure if she needed that much space. She closed the link and opened the next one.

The exterior came into view, and immediately, Brielle felt something shift in her chest. This house was a single-story ranch, painted a soft gray with white trim. A small but inviting front porch sat beneath a simple overhang, with two porch lights. The driveway curved gently to the side of the house, leading to a one-car garage that was attached. The yard was smaller than the first house, which would be better for her to manage. The landscaping was simple with only a few shrubs and flowers lining the front of the home.

"This feels cozy," she whispered.

She clicked inside. The front door opened directly into an open concept living space. The living room flowed seamlessly into the dining area and kitchen, all on the same level, with luxury vinyl plank flooring that mimicked hardwood but looked softer, warmer. The walls were painted a light beige, and recessed lighting gave the space an airy feel even without sunlight streaming in. The living room wasn't huge, but it was just the right size for her and the baby. It was big enough for a comfortable couch, a loveseat, and a media stand without feeling crowded. She could already imagine curling up there, pregnancy pillow tucked behind her back, watching late-night TV with her feet propped up.

The kitchen was compact but modern – white cabinets with black hardware, subway tile backsplash, and new appliances. There was a breakfast bar with room for two stools instead of a formal dining room, and Brielle loved it. Even from just looking at the pictures, this felt like it was her home. She clicked through to the hallway, which led to two bedrooms and a bathroom. The primary bedroom was at the back of the house, overlooking the backyard. It wasn't huge, but it was comfortable, enough room for a queen-sized bed, a dresser, and a small sitting area by the window. The closet wasn't massive, but it was deep enough for all her clothes and shoes. And even though the en-suite bathroom didn't have a tub, it did have a walk-in shower with a built-in bench.

The second bedroom was smaller, clearly meant to be a child's room or a home office. Sunlight streamed in through a single window, and the walls were painted a soft neutral tone. Her eyes lingered there longer than anywhere else. She could see it, a crib against one wall, a changing table on another, and a small dresser. *This is my son's room,* she thought. The main bathroom was updated too, with a tub-shower combo and modern fixtures. Just like the first house, the tour ended in the backyard, which was fenced and modest but had a small concrete patio just off the back door. It was perfect for sitting outside with a book and a glass of wine when the weather was nice. Brielle closed the tour and just sat there for a moment, her hand resting protectively over her stomach.

The decision came easy to her. The second house wasn't flashy or as big as the first one. However, to Brielle, it felt like home. It was on one level, so she didn't have to worry about climbing stairs while she was on bed rest. With it being smaller, it would also be easier for her to maintain. And most of all, it felt like the place she couldn't wait to start over in. She placed a call to Taj, and he answered almost immediately.

"Hey, Bri, did you get a chance to look at the houses yet?"

"Yes, I did. I took the tour for both of them."

"Okay, great. So, what did you think?" he asked.

"I liked them both, but I want the second one," she said without hesitation.

He chuckled softly. "That fast, huh?"

"I didn't even have to think about it," Brielle admitted. "The first house was beautiful, but the second one felt more like me. It's just going to be me and the baby, so I feel like the first house is just too big."

"Yeah, I thought that too, but I still wanted you to see them both. I'll call my homeboy right now and let him know. Then, I'll call you back with the details."

"Thank you so much, Taj. I really appreciate you."

"It's no problem, Brielle. If I can help you out, then I'm for sure going to do it."

Brielle smiled, thanking Taj again, before ending the call. She walked down to the kitchen and made herself something to eat before settling on the couch and watching TV for the rest of the night.

Chapter Thirteen

Taj sat across from Rich in his home office, the sunlight shining in through the floor-to-ceiling windows. Rich leaned back in his chair, tablet in hand, scrolling through documents. It was Wednesday afternoon, and Taj was already ten steps ahead, as he put his plan into motion.

"You sure about this?" Rich asked, finally breaking the silence. "I mean, the house is solid, neighborhood is good. But that shit small as hell. You really want to buy this shit?"

Taj looked him in the eye, showing that this wasn't a game. "It's the one she wants."

Rich studied him for a second. "I thought you said she wanted to rent it?"

Taj didn't flinch. "She does."

"Then why are you buying it? You don't strike me as the secret sugar daddy type."

"I'm not," Taj said calmly. "That's why she can't know."

Rich set the tablet down. "Okay, walk me through this. What the fuck are we doing?"

Taj exhaled, rubbing his palm over his beard. "She thinks she's renting from you for a thousand a month with a one year lease. I need you to draw up a standard lease, just like you would for any other tenant."

Rich raised a brow. "And the rent money? Where is that going to go?"

"Every dollar she gives you goes directly into a high interest savings account. I don't want her to know anything until I tell her, so I need you to play your part as a landlord. If something is broken and she calls you, just call me, and I'll send someone. She's good people, and she's been through a lot. I just want to make sure she's straight."

Rich let out a low whistle. "You're serious about this shit?"

"Dead ass," Taj replied. "She's been through enough. I just want to make sure that she never goes through what she went through again. I'll throw in ten thousand above your asking price for this. I just feel the need to protect her, and this is how I plan to do it."

"Oh, you love her." Rich chuckled. "You lucky you my boy because I damn sure ain't doing all this shit for anybody else," Rich continued.

Taj didn't answer right away. His mind drifted to Brielle's soft smile. "I care," he said finally. "Enough to make sure she and that baby never feel unstable again."

"Alright, you seem to have everything figured out, I guess."

They sat in silence for a moment before Rich tapped the tablet again. "Alright. Lease will say renter pays utilities and standard maintenance. With a one-year option to renew. I'll go set the savings account up tomorrow."

"Perfect. Sounds like a plan. I'll have the money wired to you by the end of the day," Taj assured before walking out of Rich's office and leaving his house. Although the sun was high in the sky, it was still cold in Detroit with it being the beginning of April. Everything was all set. Once he wired the money to Rich, Brielle would be the owner of her new home and would never have to live with anyone else ever again. He smiled to himself, as he got into his Range Rover and headed home.

A week later, it was moving day for Brielle, and Taj seemed to wake up before the sun did. He was so excited that he hadn't done much sleeping the night before. He took a shower and dressed before heading down to the kitchen to make himself a quick breakfast. He'd hired movers to retrieve Brielle's things from Amya's house and move them into her new house and would have to meet them there at nine. So, after he was done eating, he washed the few breakfast dishes, slid into his coat, and walked out the door. After putting Amya's address into his GPS, he was on his way.

When he pulled up to Amya's house about twenty minutes later, the movers were already there. Amya had let them in, and they had started loading the truck. He walked up the steps and knocked on the front door, smiling when Brielle opened it.

"Good morning, Bri. Are you excited about today?" he asked, as he walked into the house.

"I am. I'm so happy to finally have my own place again," Brielle replied, placing her hand on her protruding belly. "You know you didn't have to come over here. Everything is already boxed and ready for the movers."

"I wanted to. I don't want any stress on you today, so I'm going to handle everything. And that includes supervising the movers every step of the way."

"Thank you," Brielle said with a smile.

Taj handled business, making sure the movers handled everything with care and packed the truck with all of Brielle's belongings before they headed to Brielle's new house. Brielle rode over with Taj, and Amya let her know that she would be over a little later to help her unpack. On the drive over, Brielle kept apologizing to Taj for not being able to help. However, Taj shrugged it off.

"You're not lifting a finger," he told her. "I hired the movers to do the bulk of the work. And everything they don't do, me, Amya, and yo' mama will."

"You're amazing, Taj. I don't know how I got so lucky to get a friend like you."

Taj smiled, thinking back on the day he'd met Brielle, the one accident that now seemed more like fate to him. From that moment, he felt protective of Brielle without even knowing why. To Taj, it felt like it was his responsibility to ensure she was going to be okay. He wasn't stupid. He knew Brielle was pregnant by another man. He'd known that from the beginning. But what stood out to him wasn't the pregnancy; it was his absence. It was clear to Taj that whoever the man was, he didn't give a damn about Brielle or the baby; however, Taj did.

The moment they got to the house and Brielle opened the door; the movers began unloading their truck and placing everything inside the house, putting every item exactly where Brielle told them it went. Taj had paid them extra to put together all of her furniture, so that was one less thing they would have to do. Taj moved through the house like he was on a mission. Every now and then, he'd catch Brielle watching him with a smile on her face.

By early afternoon, the last box was unloaded, and the furniture had been assembled. Taj stood in the doorway of the living room, happy that he'd been able to help Brielle with her new beginning. He heard her when she walked up from behind, and he turned to face her.

"I can't believe I'm finally in my own home. I feel like I can finally breathe," Brielle spoke, looking up at Taj. "Thank you, Taj. For everything."

He shrugged. "I just want to make sure you're straight."

She smiled at him. "And that's what makes you a wonderful person."

The movers were loading the last of their equipment back into the truck when Taj stepped outside to sign off on everything. He started unpacking boxes and putting away dishes, as he waited for Denise and Amya to come help. He'd told Brielle that she was to do nothing but sit on the couch and watch TV, and he meant that. He wasn't going to allow her to lift a finger. He stood in the kitchen, hanging pictures, when his stomach began to growl. Pulling his phone from his pocket, he opened the DoorDash app, knowing that Chinese was Brielle's favorite.

He'd just finished ordering the food when he heard Denise and Amya enter the house. Taj walked into the living room, greeting both of them. He watched as Brielle stood from the couch and walked over to them, embracing them both.

"This house is so nice. It's just right for you and the baby," Denise complimented.

"Thanks, Mama. That's exactly what I said when I saw it. I can't wait to decorate his room."

"Yeah, well, we gonna have to get on the ball with that. He's gonna be here in about six weeks."

"I know. I'm going to start ordering things for him this week," Brielle replied.

Amya moved through the house, looking at things and nodding her head in approval.

"This is nice, and it's not too far from me and Mama D. I'm happy for you, best friend," Amya uttered.

"I hope you all are hungry because I ordered Chinese," Taj chimed in.

"Oh, wow," Amya murmured. "You hired movers, set up the whole house, and ordered dinner?"

Taj chuckled lightly. "She's on bed rest and couldn't do it, so somebody had to."

Amya tilted her head, looking him up and down. "So, let me get this straight. You not even her man, but you movin' like you the husband, the baby daddy, and the Home Depot credit card? You do know she pregnant, right? So, that means you can't cash in none of them coochie coupons you rackin' up."

Brielle groaned. "Amya, please!"

Denise tried to hide it, but she couldn't, as she burst out into laughter.

Taj laughed, shaking his head. "I'm just helpin', that's all."

Amya smirked. "Uh huh. Just helping. Got it."

She stepped closer to Brielle and whispered loud enough for everyone to hear. "Girl, if this is friendship, I need to re-evaluate everybody in my phone."

"Amya, please shut the hell up." Brielle laughed. "Thank you for ordering food," Brielle spoke, turning to Taj.

"It's no problem. I was hungry, so I ordered enough for everyone."

Brielle sat back on the couch, while Taj, Denise, and Amya unpacked boxes and began putting things away. About twenty minutes later, there was a knock at the door, and Taj knew it was the food. He opened the door, grabbing the two bags, before walking back into the kitchen. Brielle called out to Amya and Denise, who were in Brielle's room, putting away her clothes. When they came out, everyone made their plates and went into the living room to eat. Denise picked out a movie, and they watched it while they ate.

Once everything was unpacked and the leftover food had been put away, Taj told Brielle he was going home. She thanked him once again, and he hugged her before he walked out the house

By the time he made it home, it was after eight in the evening. He went directly to his en-suite bathroom, peeled out his clothes, and stepped inside the shower. Although he was tired, he felt good knowing that Brielle was all set up in a house that no one could ever take away from her. When Taj was done, he dried off before walking into his room and sliding into a pair of boxers. He laid in bed and spent the rest of the night flipping through channels until he fell asleep.

Taj slept in the next morning, not waking up until well after noon. After handling his business in the bathroom, Taj made himself a smoothie and went to the gym. He usually worked out three times a week but had been slipping and hadn't been to the gym all week. He spent an hour working out before spending another thirty minutes in the sauna. The workout made him feel ten times better, and the hot shower he took when he got back home was the icing on the cake. It was Sunday, and Taj was going over his mother's house for Sunday dinner, but until it was time for him to go, he planned to chill and watch the game.

At around five that afternoon, Taj dressed in a pair of black Balmain slacks that he paired with a fitted black turtleneck. His cut was clean, and his waves were deep. He clasped a gold herringbone chain around his neck and sprayed on Initio's Oud for Greatness. Once he put on his shoes and coat, he was ready to go.

Taj pulled into his mother's driveway about thirty minutes later. Sunday dinner had always been sacred in her house, and missing three in a row had earned him more than a few guilt-laced phone calls. By the fourth one, she'd made him promise that he would be there this Sunday. The moment he opened the door; the familiar smells wrapped around him – fried chicken, candied yams, greens, and whatever else his mother had prepared. His mother's voice floated from the kitchen before he even had a chance to close the door.

"Don't stand there. Get yo' ass in here and come hug yo' mama."

He smiled, locking the door and heading her way. She pulled him into a tight embrace, hands firm on his back like she needed to feel that he was really there. Taj's mother, Rita, was fifty-five years old and stood five feet six with dark chocolate skin. She had salt and pepper hair that she kept in a stylish pixie. She wore a wine-colored dress with a matching pair of shoes. She was where her children got their style from because if Rita didn't know how to do anything else, she could dress and cook.

"I'm so glad you finally here. I ain't seen you in a month of Sundays," Rita spoke.

"I'm sorry, Mama. I just been a little busy," Taj replied.

"That's what you said last Sunday. And the one before that. And the one before that," she replied. "Which tells me exactly nothing and everything at the same time. I know that club you own ain't taking up all yo' time like that."

Before he could respond, the house filled with noise, as his nieces came barreling through the door.

"Uncle Taj!" his five-year-old niece, Maleah, yelled, running over to him. She reached up for him, and he picked her up in his arms.

"What's up, Lele? How's the smartest five-year-old in the entire world doing?"

"Good. Mommy said you wasn't coming today. But I told her you was cause Grandma made you promise, and you never break a promise."

"That's right, baby girl. You always keep your promises." Taj smiled.

Just then, his seven and nine year old nieces, Ashanti and Samia, walked into the kitchen, both smiling when they saw him. They both rushed over to him, hugging him like they hadn't seen him in years. Just then, his sister, Tati, walked in, hugging Rita before turning to Taj.

"What up doe, bro? Me and Tessa thought you wasn't coming. I was 'bout to show up at yo' house if you wasn't here today." Tati laughed, walking over to Taj and hugging him.

"Where is Tessa at anyway?" Taj asked.

"She in the living room changing Chloe's clothes. That little girl spilled a whole cup of juice on herself." Tati laughed and shook her head. "In my niece's defense though, it was Tessa's fault because she didn't close her sippy cup all the way."

A few minutes later, Tessa walked in the kitchen holding Chloe in her arms. Chloe's little face lit up the moment she saw Taj. He reached for her, and she damn near jumped out of Tessa's arms trying to get to him.

"You finally decided to show up, huh?" Tessa uttered the moment he took Chloe from her arms. "Mama was about to put out a missing person's report on yo' ass."

"Damn, a dude miss a few Sunday dinners, and y'all acting like I just abandoned the family," Taj joked. "I just been busy, that's all."

Tati raised an eyebrow. "Do busy got a name?"

Taj shook his head. "You messy."

"Don't act like Tati ain't right, Taj. I know my son. You ain't been around in weeks, so I already know what that means. We ain't telling you to bring her over for dinner next Sunday; we just asking you what her name is."

Before Taj could say anything, Tessa's husband, Hendrix, came walking into the kitchen, saving the day without even knowing. It wasn't that Taj was ashamed of Brielle because he wasn't. He just knew they were only friends and didn't need his family making it into something it wasn't.

"What up doe? You good, bro?" Hendrix asked, slapping hands with Taj.

"What up doe? I can't call it. Just living life day by day."

Hendrix nodded. "I feel you on that. That's all we can do."

They stood in the kitchen, talking for a few more minutes, before Rita told everyone that the food was ready. They made their way into the dining room and gathered around the table. Taj blessed the food, while the rest of the family bowed their heads. When he was done, everyone made their plates and sat down to eat. Taj sat back for a moment, watching his family – the way Hendrix cut up the meat for his youngest daughter, the way Tessa nudged him playfully when he stole a piece of chicken from her plate. They had been together for over twelve years and were still so happy together. They had a love that Taj admired and wanted to achieve in his own life.

He'd built businesses, stacked money, made sure he'd never struggle the way he'd seen others do. But sitting there, watching the love of companionship right before his eyes, he knew all that he had was nothing without someone to share it with – someone to come home to and hold every night. At thirty, Taj was successful but had not yet found that one woman to share his wealth with. Rita caught his eyes and smiled, leaning in a little closer to Taj.

"Are you gonna tell me her name?"

Taj blinked. "Tell you whose name?"

"The girl that got you all quiet," she replied. "The one taking all your time but you didn't bring to Sunday dinner."

"Ma, there is no girl. I have a new friend, but that's all we are."

"Mmhmm. That's what men always say right before they fall headfirst."

Tati smirked. "Is she pretty?"

"Does she treat you right is the real question?" Tessa added.

Taj pushed back from the table slightly, shaking his head. "Y'all doing too much. I said we friends. That's all; that's it."

But even as he said it, Brielle's face flashed in his mind. He wanted to tell Tati that she was beautiful and took his breath away every time he saw her. He wanted to tell Tessa that he felt his best when he was with her. But instead, he remained silent and continued to eat his food.

When dinner was over, Taj helped his mother clear the table and load the dishwasher. She made him a to-go plate filled with all his favorites, and before he walked out the house, he promised his mother that he'd be there next Sunday for dinner. Getting into his Rover, he drove home with nothing but thoughts of Brielle running through his mind.

Chapter Fourteen

One Saturday afternoon, Taj found himself pulling up in front of Brielle's house with two paint cans carefully wedged in the backseat, along with rollers, drop cloths, and everything else they needed. She'd sent him a picture of the paint swatches the night before, soft, calming tones of blue perfect for a baby. He'd went to Home Depot and got the exact paint she'd sent him. He grabbed the bags and paint and got out his truck. He walked up the walkway and knocked on the door.

The door opened almost immediately, and Brielle stood there in leggings and an oversized t-shirt. Her long box braids were pulled back in a low ponytail, and she looked extremely comfortable and even more beautiful.

"Hey," she greeted, smiling wide when she saw him.

"Hey, yourself. I got all the goods." Taj held up his hands to show Brielle the items. "Damn, and you got it smelling good up in here."

She laughed. "I figured we should eat before we start painting. I didn't want you passing out on me, so I made us breakfast."

Taj placed the bags down on the floor then followed her toward the kitchen, already knowing whatever she'd made was going to be delicious. The table was already set with plates stacked with fluffy scrambled eggs, sausage, golden hash browns, and thick slices of French toast dusted lightly with powdered sugar. A bowl of fresh strawberries sat in the center, along with orange juice and coffee.

"Damn, you did all this? You're supposed to be on bed rest, young lady."

"I been on bed rest, but shit, I gotta eat. Plus, I'm ready to give birth anyway. This load getting too heavy to keep carrying it around," she joked.

Taj laughed, and they both took their seats at the table. Brielle poured both of them a glass of orange juice, and Taj thanked her for cooking.

Brielle shrugged. "It's the least I can do seeing how you're helping me with the nursery."

"You know if you call then I'm coming." Taj smiled.

As they ate, Brielle told him about the way she envisioned setting up the nursery. And Taj listened to every little detail. He could tell she was getting more and more excited about the baby's arrival with each passing day, and so was he. Even though the baby wasn't his, he was still going to be there for him just as he'd been for Brielle. He didn't know the details about what happened between her and her child's father, but Taj knew he wasn't around, and Taj hated men like that. He never understood how a man could get a woman pregnant and then leave her to raise the baby.

After they finished eating, Brielle stood and grabbed the plates. Taj moved to help, but she shook her head.

"I got it, Taj. It's only two plates."

Taj laughed and nodded his head. When she was done washing the breakfast dishes, they headed down the hall toward the room that would soon belong to her son. The nursery was empty except for a crib still in its box and a small dresser that sat in the middle of the room, away from the walls they were about to paint. Brielle leaned against the doorframe, one hand resting on her stomach, looking around with a soft smile.

"I can't believe in just a few short weeks, my son will be here. I'm about to be somebody's mama."

Taj set the paint cans down and glanced at her. "You're going to be a great mama to that little boy. You already are, and he's not even here yet."

"Thank you for that, Taj. It really means a lot." She looked at him then smiled again. "Let's paint before I start crying."

Taj laughed. "Say less."

As he laid out the drop cloths and popped open the first can of paint, Taj realized he wasn't just helping her set up a nursery. He was building something with her. Whether either of them was ready to name it yet or not, they were making memories. They began painting, Taj looking over at Brielle every now and then to make sure she was doing okay. Each time he looked at her, he saw her smiling.

After they finished cleaning up the brushes and sealing the paint cans, the room was left to dry, the soft new color already changing the feel of the room. Taj followed Brielle into the living room, both of them tired and ready to sit down. They settled onto the couch, Brielle tucking her legs beneath her, while Taj stretched out beside her. Without much thought, she leaned into him, her head resting against his chest. Taj stiffened for half a second then relaxed, carefully placing his arm around her.

She scrolled through different apps. "We should start a series together, something neither of us have seen and that we'll only watch together," Brielle suggested.

"Sounds good to me. Do you have a series in mind?"

"I saw a few on Netflix that I never watched. If you want, we can pick from those."

Taj nodded, and Brielle opened Netflix. She went through the list and found the series she'd added to it. She stopped on *The Blacklist* before looking over at Taj. He told her that he'd ever seen it before, and she pressed play on the first episode. The moment the episode started, they were all in with action taking off in the first five minutes.

"Oh, this shit 'bout to be good," Taj voiced, eyes locked on the TV.

Halfway through the second episode, Brielle shifted slightly, her hand resting against Taj stomach, completely unaware of what that small touch did to him. Taj stared at the TV, forcing himself to focus, reminding himself to breathe and keep it respectful. However, the more she laid there, the more he wanted to take her to her room, pregnant and all, and show her exactly how he felt about her. However, he kept his eyes on the TV.

By the end of the fifth episode, Taj told Brielle that he thought the paint was dry enough for them to go in and set everything up. She nodded, sitting up on the couch, before standing to her feet, her huge, round belly standing out straight in front of her. Taj stood as well before they both walked back into the room. Brielle opened one of the drawers in the dresser and pulled out a small toolbox and handed it to Taj.

"Thank you," he replied, taking the toolbox before opening the box the crib came in.

He began pulling out each piece one by one and setting them off to the side before taking the box and sitting it in the hallway. He worked carefully, wanting to ensure he put everything together correctly. About an hour later, Taj stepped back from the crib, tightening the last screw and giving it a firm shake to make sure it was solid.

"Alright," he voiced with satisfaction. "That thing not going nowhere. Built like a Ford truck."

Brielle laughed from the closet, sliding tiny hangers across the rod. Little onesies, sleepers, and miniature hoodies were lined up by color. "Good. I can't be having my son breakin' out of his crib in the middle of the night."

Taj glanced over his shoulder at her, smiling. "You almost done over there?" he asked.

"Yeah, I just..."

Her sentence was cut off by a sharp intake of breath followed by a small gasp. He turned just in time to see Brielle bend forward, one hand flying to her stomach, the other bracing against the closet wall.

"Brielle?" His tone changed instantly. "What's wrong?"

She straightened slightly, eyes wide, face pale. For half a

second, she looked confused. Then, she looked down at the floor. "Oh, my God," she whispered.

Taj crossed the room. "What? What is it?"

She swallowed hard, panic creeping into her voice. "Taj... my stomach. I think... I think my water just broke." She winced again, another wave of pain rolling through her. "I think I'm in labor." Her eyes filled with tears, as she looked up at him.

For a moment, the room froze, and Taj's mouth hung open. Then reality slammed into him all at once. *Fuck, she's having the baby,* he thought. "Okay," he spoke calmly even though his heart was pounding. "Okay. We good. Calm down and just breathe."

He grabbed his phone off the dresser, hands steady despite the adrenaline rushing through him. He gently wrapped an arm around her waist, supporting her, as they headed toward the door. Brielle leaned into him, trusting him completely, and that trust hit him harder than the panic ever could.

"I need my hospital bag. It's in that closet." Brielle pointed.

Taj nodded, steadying her against the couch, before rushing over to the closet and grabbing the light blue duffle bag. He rushed back over to her, and they walked out the house. He didn't remember much about the drive to the hospital. All he remembered was the sound of Brielle's breathing and the way her fingers dug into his hand between contractions. She was in pain, and Taj tried his best to get to the hospital as quickly as possible.

Brielle had placed calls to both her mother and Amya, her voice shaky but strong, as she told them what was happening. Taj stayed focused, one hand on the wheel, the other gripping hers whenever she reached for him.

"You doing good," he kept telling her. "I got you. We almost there."

When they pulled up to the hospital entrance, Taj jumped out the car immediately, rushing to the other side and opening her door. A nurse spotted them instantly, rushing over to them with a wheelchair.

"My water broke," Brielle uttered through clenched teeth, as another contraction hit.

Taj stayed right by her side, as they wheeled Brielle through the doors, never once letting go of her hand. When they took her back to the labor and delivery unit, he walked alongside the bed like he was the father of the baby she was carrying. The nurses moved quickly, hooking Brielle up to monitors and checking her vitals. Taj stood at her side, murmuring reassurances into her ear.

"You good?" he asked softly.

She nodded, tears in her eyes. "I'm scared, Taj."

"I know," he said honestly. "But you're doing so good."

About fifteen minutes later, the door swung open, and Denise rushed in first, her face tight with concern. Amya followed right behind her, already emotional.

"Oh, my baby," Denise spoke, moving to Brielle's side, taking her other hand.

"I'm here too, best friend," Amya added quickly.

Brielle let out a shaky breath, relief washing over her, as she looked around the room – her mother on one side, her best friend on the other, and Taj still right there, unwavering. Taj stepped back just enough to give them space, but he never left the room. He leaned against the wall for a moment, watching Brielle through it all, the pain, her strength, and the way she squeezed her mother's hand then looked back at him like she needed to make sure he was still there. Taj stood there, watching Brielle's body tense, as another contraction rolled through her, and every instinct in him screamed to *do something*, fix it, take it away, hell, even carry it for her, but he couldn't. This was a pain that he couldn't lift off her shoulders, no matter how strong he was. And that fucked with him inside.

His chest felt tight, almost aching, as he watched her grip the rails of the bed, her face pinched with pain and her breathing uneven. Each sound she made hit him harder than any punch ever could. If he could've traded places with her, taken even a fraction of what she was feeling, he would've done it without hesitation. So instead, he leaned closer, trying to comfort her as best he could.

"I know. I know," he spoke softly, his voice steady even

though his insides were anything but. "Breathe, Brielle. In through your nose, slow, then out through your mouth. I'm right here. We all are."

Brielle nodded her head, breathing the way he told her to.

"That's it," he coached gently when another contraction built. "You stronger than this. Let it come, you can't stop them. You just gotta breathe through it." He spoke as he wiped sweat from her forehead.

Every time she cried out, Taj felt it in his chest. He counted her breaths with her, trying to keep her focused. Denise was on the other side of her, coaching Brielle in her own way, while Amya sat in the chair, just staring. She looked like she didn't have a clue what to do, and neither did he. However, Taj wasn't going to let it show.

Five hours into labor, the room had settled into a tense rhythm – monitors beeping, nurses coming and going, and Brielle drifting between moments of strength and exhaustion. Denise glanced over at Brielle, telling her that she needed to go grab a cup of coffee. Taj heard her and spoke up, telling her that he could use a cup as well. He looked over at Brielle and told her he would be right back. She smiled and nodded her head.

The hospital's Starbucks was busy, the smell of coffee thick in the air. Taj ordered quickly, his mind on getting back to Brielle as quickly as possible. Denise stood beside him, quiet for a moment longer than usual. Once they stepped aside to wait for their drinks, she finally spoke.

"You care about my daughter, don't you?" Denise asked, looking up at Taj.

Taj exhaled slowly, rubbing the back of his neck. "Yeah, I do."

Denise turned to face him fully then, mother's eyes sharp but not unkind. "So, tell me what you're doing with her, Taj. Because I see you. I see how you show up, and it's more than any friend I've ever had."

He didn't rush his answer as he spoke. "I like Brielle a lot. But I know she's been through some things, and her life not exactly simple right now." He shook his head slightly. "So, I'm happy being whatever Brielle needs me to be right now."

Denise studied him closely. "And the baby?"

"Her being pregnant don't change how I feel about her. If anything, it makes me want to be there for her even more," he said without hesitation. "I know the father ain't around. But that ain't my place to fill unless Brielle ever wanted that. I just want to be there for her in whatever way she needs."

For a long moment, Denise didn't say anything. Then, her shoulders relaxed, just a bit. "You know," she said quietly, "a lot of men say the right things. But very few actually *do* the right things."

Taj met her gaze. "That's exactly why I let my actions do the talking."

Their names were called, letting them know their orders were ready. Taj walked up and took them both before handing one to Denise before they walked out of the coffee shop. They headed back toward the elevators, coffee in hand, ready to get back to Brielle's side. When they made it back to Brielle's room, the energy had shifted completely. A doctor stood at the foot of the bed, calm but focused, while a nurse adjusted the monitors.

"Brielle," the doctor said, smiling reassuringly. "You're fully dilated. It's time."

Amya was already at her side, holding her hand, eyes wide with emotion. "You hear that? It's go time, bestie. Our little man is about to enter this world."

Taj's heart slammed against his chest, as he moved back into position beside Brielle, Denise taking the other side next to Amya. Brielle looked overwhelmed, scared, and strong all at once. And Taj was going to make sure she held it together.

"I can't do this," she whispered, tears slipping from the corners of her eyes.

"Yes, you can," Taj encouraged, his voice steady. He leaned close, so she could hear him over everything else. "You doing amazing. You're so strong."

When the first push came, Brielle cried out, gripping Taj's

hand with everything she had. He didn't flinch, as she squeezed his hand tightly.

"You got this, best friend. Push that baby out," Amya coached.

Each contraction seemed to bring her more pain than the last, but Taj never stopped talking her through it. Denise prayed softly under her breath. Then, the final push came, and a sharp cry filled the room. The doctor smiled wide, holding the baby up and placing him onto Brielle's chest.

"Congratulations, Mom. It's a boy."

Brielle sobbed openly, her body trembling with exhaustion and relief, as she cradled him in her arms. "My baby," Brielle whispered, kissing his forehead before counting his fingers and toes. "Thank you, God."

"What's his name?" the nurse asked gently.

Brielle looked down at him before looking back at the nurse. "Nisaiah," she replied firmly.

Taj felt his breath catch. Watching Brielle bring Nisaiah into the world was something Taj knew he would carry with him forever. The strength she showed, the way she fought through pain with nothing but love on the other side, humbled him. He stared at Brielle holding her son and realized this was the most beautiful thing he had ever witnessed.

Chapter Fifteen

Two months had passed since Nisaiah's birth, and Brielle still found herself in moments of disbelief. Standing in her kitchen at three in the morning, warming a bottle, rocking him to sleep in the quiet hours before dawn, still took some getting used to. Life had changed fast, but somehow, it felt right. Taj had been there for all of it. He hadn't disappeared after the hospital. He hadn't slowly faded into the background the way Nisaiah's own father had. Instead, he showed up every day in small, steady ways that mattered more than any grand gesture.

He brought groceries when she was too tired to leave the house. He held Nisaiah while Brielle showered or just needed a break. He changed diapers without being asked, learned how Nisaiah liked to be rocked, learned which cry meant hunger and which one meant he just wanted to be held. Taj treated Nisaiah more like a son that Delano ever did. Watching Taj with her son did something to Brielle's heart she wasn't prepared for.

He never overstepped. Never tried to replace the father that wasn't in his life anyway. He simply loved Nisaiah and chose to be there for him. And now more than ever, Brielle loved being around him. She loved the way he made her laugh when Nisaiah had her running on no sleep. The way he listened when she talked about motherhood fears she didn't feel safe saying out loud to anyone else. The way he looked at her, not just as a mother but as a woman. Somewhere between late-night feedings and early-morning coffee runs, something shifted inside her.

At first, she told herself it was just gratitude, maybe even comfort. But the truth became harder to ignore with each passing day. She wanted more than friendship with Taj but wasn't sure if he wanted the same. She wanted to reach for his hand without overthinking. Wanted to lean into him without reminding herself of lines she'd drawn when things felt too complicated. But most of all, she wanted to know what it would feel like to be chosen by him. Sometimes, she caught herself watching Taj across the room while he played with Nisaiah, a soft smile on his face, and she would pretend they were a family. That she was his wife and Nisaiah was their son.

Brielle had spent months protecting her heart by telling herself friendship was enough. But as Taj continued to show up both consistently and patiently, she was starting to realize that maybe the danger wasn't wanting more but pretending that she didn't.

Saturday afternoon sunlight spilled softly through the windows when Taj came through the front door. He didn't call out for Brielle, not since Nisaiah was born. Instead, just like always, he kicked off his shoes and headed straight down the hall to the nursery. Brielle watched from the doorway, arms folded loosely across her chest. She laughed, shaking her head, before closing the door and following Taj. Nisaiah was asleep in his crib, fists curled near his face, chest rising and falling in a steady rhythm. Taj leaned over the crib, smiling to himself.

"Hey, lil' man," he whispered.

Carefully, he slid his hands beneath Nisaiah and lifted him out, cradling him against his chest. The baby stirred but didn't cry, just let out a soft sound before settling again. Taj gently rocked him.

"I just wanted to say hello," he murmured.

Brielle felt something warm spread through her chest, as she watched him. This man had no obligation, no title, no requirement to love her child the way he did. Yet here he was, whispering to her son like the world stopped when he held him. After a moment, Taj carefully laid Nisaiah back into the crib, tucking the blanket around him with practiced care. He stood there for a second longer than necessary, just watching him sleep. Only then did he turn around and notice Brielle standing there. She smiled at him, her eyes shining, as she looked at him.

"Well, good afternoon," she whispered.

"My bad, Bri. I was just so excited to see Nisaiah. You good?"

"Yeah," Brielle whispered. "I'm better than good."

"Me too," Taj replied, as they stepped out of the nursery. "Two months already," he spoke quietly. "That don't even feel like it's been that long."

Brielle smiled, as she followed him into the living room. "Tell me about it. I swear I just brought him home yesterday."

They settled into their usual spots on the couch, the baby monitor placed right in the center of the coffee table, so they could hear Nisaiah when he woke up. Brielle picked up the remote and opened Netflix, already knowing exactly where she was going. They were now on season six of *The Blacklist*.

"I've been waiting on you for two days to see what's going to happen after that last episode. And since we promised to only watch it together, I had to wait on you," she revealed. "As much as I wanted to watch it, I couldn't cheat on you like that."

Taj chuckled. "Well, I'm glad you didn't cheat."

Brielle hit play, the familiar theme music filling the room. She curled her legs beneath her, instinctively leaning closer to Taj, their shoulders brushing. They were both locked on the screen, as the episode played. Every now and then, Brielle glanced at the baby monitor, comforted by the steady image of Nisaiah sleeping peacefully. She caught Taj's eyes doing the same, and she couldn't help but smile to herself. As the next episode began, Brielle laid her head on Taj's shoulder, as they watched. Halfway into the second episode, Taj shifted beside her.

"You hungry?" he asked casually, eyes still on the screen.

Brielle didn't even hesitate. She nodded once, already smiling. "Yeah."

At the exact same time, they both spoke. "Chinese." They froze then looked at each other before laughing.

"See," Taj chuckled, pointing his finger at Brielle, "that's how I know we spend too much time together." She grabbed her phone and went to the DoorDash app, but Taj stopped her. "I can order it."

Brielle smiled and shook her head. "You always pay for the food. I got it this time."

Taj nodded, and she placed the order from their usual spot. When she set the phone down, she leaned back against the couch, letting out a small sigh.

"Man," she uttered, almost to herself, "I would love a glass of wine right now. Or two."

Taj turned to her, studying her face. "You want me to run to the liquor store?"

She looked at him, surprised by how quickly he offered, then nodded. "Yeah, if you don't mind."

"Mind?" He shook his head and reached for his key fob. "I got you."

As he stood, Brielle watched him for a second longer than necessary. She paused the episode, as Taj walked out the door. She glanced at the baby monitor again. Nisaiah's soft fussing drifted through the monitor, pulling Brielle off the couch almost immediately. She padded down the hallway, already knowing that cry. She flicked on the small lamp in the nursery, keeping the light low, as she lifted him from his crib. His face scrunched for a second before relaxing against her chest, his tiny fingers curling into the fabric of her shirt.

"I know. Mama's got you," she whispered.

She walked into the kitchen and prepared a bottle before walking back into the nursery. She settled into the rocking chair and fed him, watching his eyelids flutter, as he drank. Moments like this still amazed her, how something so small could completely grab hold of her heart. Once he finished, Brielle changed his diaper, her movements gentle and practiced. Nisaiah barely protested, letting out a small grunt before relaxing again. By the time she laid him back in his crib, his eyes were already closed.

Brielle stood there a little longer, just looking at him. Two months ago, everything in her life had shifted. And somehow, Taj had been right there for all of it. She turned off the lamp and quietly closed the door behind her, heading back toward the living room right as she heard the front door open. She looked up at him, automatically smiling, as he walked into the kitchen to chill the wine.

Taj sat back on the couch, and Brielle pressed play before getting comfortable. Within minutes, they were both locked in. Brielle found herself leaning slightly toward him without thinking, her shoulder brushing his arm. Taj didn't move away. If anything, he shifted just enough that their sides stayed connected. She tried to focus on the screen, but her awareness of him was louder than the dialogue.

The doorbell rang, and Brielle knew it was the food. She went to get up, but before she could, Taj walked to the door and grabbed the food, the smell of Chinese instantly filling the room. Taj set the bag on the coffee table and opened it, handing Brielle her container and a fork, before taking his and sitting back on the couch. They ate with their eyes locked on the screen.

Once they were done, Taj gathered the empty containers and took them into the kitchen. Brielle heard cabinets open and close then the soft clink of glass. When he came back, he had a bottle of red wine in one hand and two glasses in the other. He poured carefully, not filling them too much, and handed one to her. Brielle took a sip, savoring it. The taste felt familiar and foreign all at once. By the time she was halfway through the glass, warmth had already started to bloom in her chest, her shoulders loosening, her thoughts feeling lighter. She giggled and sipped a few more times, and Taj looked over at her.

"You good?" he asked quietly, glancing down at her.

"Mm-hmm," she murmured. "I feel very relaxed."

The baby monitor crackled a few minutes later, followed by Nisaiah's soft fussing. Brielle started to sit up, but Taj gently placed his hand on her arm. "I got him," he announced without hesitation. "Just pause the show."

She watched him disappear down the hall, her heart fluttering softly, as she watched him step into the role so naturally. No matter how many times he did it, it always surprised her. Taj didn't hesitate with her son, just always showed up. About fifteen minutes later, Taj was walking back into the living room. Taj sat back down, closer this time. Brielle could smell his cologne, as she leaned into him. Her glass was empty now, and she realized she felt a bit tipsy.

She turned to him, eyes a little heavy. "Thank you," she uttered.

"For what?" Taj asked, confused.

"For just being you." The words slipped out before she could stop them.

Taj held her gaze, something unspoken passing between them. The room felt smaller suddenly, and Brielle knew, tipsy or not, that this was starting to feel like more than friendship. So, she didn't stop herself when she leaned in. The moment his lips met hers again, everything else faded, and all that mattered was them. His lips were soft, and his hands were steady, as they roamed her body.

"Brielle," he murmured against her mouth, pulling back just enough to search her face. "You sure?"

She nodded, her heart racing. "Yes."

Taj nodded, leaning back into the kiss. He scooped her up effortlessly, and Brielle looped her arms around his neck, as he carried her down the hallway. The bedroom felt warmer the moment they stepped inside, quieter, like the rest of the world had been shut out. He laid her gently on the bed, his touch careful and reverent, as if she were something precious. For a moment, they just looked at each other. Two people who had danced around their feelings for far too long finally stood in the truth of what had been building between them.

Taj slid off her sweatpants effortlessly, her legs spread so that he could position himself between them. He kissed her softly, gently caressing her face. When they separated, Taj eased himself down the bed, positioning his face between her legs, his hands lightly gripping her thighs. She gasped the moment his tongue touched her. Her eyes closed, and she leaned up just enough to remove her shirt. Her toes curled, as she placed one leg over his shoulder.

"I been waiting to taste you, and you just as sweet as I thought you would be," Taj whispered between licks and gentle sucks.

His hands roamed her body, as his tongue played with her clit, causing sounds she'd never heard before to escape her lips. She placed her hand on his head, pushing him in deep, as she grinded in slow circles. She'd never been this wet before, and just when she thought Taj couldn't make her feel any better, he slid two fingers inside her.

"Taj," she moaned, opening her legs even wider.

"That's right, baby. Keep my name rollin' off that tongue."

The dual sensation of Taj's tongue on her clit while his fingers penetrated inside her sent shockwaves running through her body. When he finally lifted his head, he kept his fingers inside her, as he kissed up her stomach. He moved his fingers in slow circles, as he continued to place gentle kisses on her skin. When his lips touched her nipples, she gasped once more. He sucked and twirled his tongue before making his way back down to her love box.

Taj licked and sucked on Brielle as if she were his last meal. When she climaxed, he made sure to lick his plate clean. Taj stood and removed his clothes, never taking his eyes off of her. He took a condom from his pocket and rolled it on his thick manhood before tossing the gold wrapper onto the floor. Taj grabbed Brielle by the ankle and pulled her to the edge of the bed before lifting both her legs and placing them onto his shoulders. She moaned loudly, as he entered her, his thickness filling her to capacity.

"Fuckkkk. You so wet," Taj whispered into her ear.

And she was too. She could hear the gushy sounds she made,

as Taj moved around inside of her. Brielle moaned, as Taj inched in deeper, burying his face in her neck. When he pulled out and flipped her over, Brielle got on all fours, burying her face in the pillow, as he entered her from the back. They both moaned, as they found their rhythm. Sounds of skin slapping together filled the room.

"That's right, baby, get that dick," Taj coached.

Brielle, doing as she was told, arched her back deeper, as she moved her hips in slow circles, his long, thick manhood hitting her spot every time she made a full circle. He slapped her ass cheek, and she bit her pillow to stifle her moans. As long as she'd waited, she had no clue it would be this good. But it was, and Brielle wanted more.

She lifted herself, stretching out her arms for support. Taj grabbed her shoulders, leaning her back, as his manhood deepened inside her. He leaned in, his lips lightly touching her ear.

"You takin' all this dick, huh?" he whispered.

"Yesss, baby. And it feels so good," Brielle replied.

"That's a good girl."

Smack! His hand slapped her ass cheek once more.

"Take this dick like the good girl you are," he continued.

Brielle could feel the tip of his manhood swelling inside her, and she knew he was about to cum. Picking up her rhythm, she bounced back until both of their moans filled the room, as they climaxed together. Taj leaned against her, breath heavy and still inside her. Brielle welcomed him, as she continued to clench around his manhood.

"Damn," Taj moaned, planting a kiss on the nape of her neck.

He pulled out gently before getting up and going to the bathroom. Brielle lay there for a moment, still in awe of what had just happened. When Taj returned from the bathroom, Brielle went in. After she freshened up, she wrapped herself in her robe and went to go check on Nisaiah. She smiled when she saw him still sleeping peacefully in his crib. When she made her way back into her room, she saw that Taj was already dressed.

"You wanna go back into the living room and watch some more *Blacklist*?" he asked.

"Sure do." She smiled.

They walked back into the living room and sat on the couch. They'd forgotten to pause the series, so Brielle had to go back a couple of episodes until she found where they'd left off. They cuddled on the couch, as they watched the episode. Brielle looked up at him and smiled.

"I hope you know we together now after that," she voiced.

"I hope you know we was already together. I was just waiting on you to confirm it," Taj replied.

Chapter Sixteen

Taj was still riding the endorphin high from the gym when his phone rang. Sweat clung to his skin, as he stepped out into the parking lot and the humid summer air. He glanced at the screen and smiled when he saw his mother's name flash across it.

"Hey, Ma," he answered, unlocking his truck.

She didn't waste time with small talk. "I'm not doing Sunday dinner this week," she said. "With the Fourth of July being this week, that's just too much cookin'. We'll pick it back up next Sunday."

Taj nodded even though she couldn't see him, tossing his gym bag onto the passenger seat. "That's cool."

There was a brief pause on the other end, the kind that told him she wasn't done yet.

"And," she added, her voice taking on that knowing tone, "I want you to bring your new girlfriend next week."

Taj froze for half a second, keys dangling in his hand. "My what?" he asked, already smiling.

"Don't play with me," she replied. "Tati already told me that you and this mystery woman have made it official. So, I think it's only right that you bring her so that we can meet her."

He leaned against the truck, the grin spreading wider across his face. *I knew I shouldn't have told Tati big mouth ass nothing*, he thought. "Alright, I'll bring her."

"Good," Rita replied, satisfied. "I'll see you next week."

They hung up, and Taj slid into the driver's seat and pulled out of the lot, his thoughts already drifting to Brielle. His family wanted to meet her, and he hoped she was ready to meet them too. Taj had never been this sure about anyone ever, and he hoped that Brielle would be in his life for many years to come. He wasn't blind to the circumstances. He knew Brielle had a newborn, but he wanted that baby just as much as he wanted her. So, introducing her to his family was the next step. He knew they would love her just as much as he did.

Taj drove home with a smile on his face, thinking about just how bright his future now was. The moment he walked into the house, he went directly to the bathroom and took a shower. After he got dressed, he sent a text to Brielle, letting her know that he was on the way. She sent a text right back, asking him to pick up some tacos from the Mexican restaurant she liked.

Taj pulled up in front of Brielle's house about forty-five minutes later with a brown paper bag of tacos warming the passenger seat. He grabbed the bag, got out the car, and jogged up the walkway to the door. Brielle must have been watching for him because she opened the door the moment he walked up.

"Hey, baby," Taj greeted with a smile.

Brielle lifted up on her toes and kissed Taj's lips. "Hey. Nisaiah is already sleeping, and I already got Netflix pulled up on the TV."

"Oh, you ready to watch *The Blacklist*, huh?"

"Hell yeah, this the last season. I'm ready to get to it."

Taj nodded and walked over to the couch, opening the bag and pulling out tacos. Brielle pressed play, and they both grabbed a taco before sitting on the couch. They watched the first episode, while they ate, and when it was over, Taj looked at her.

"My family wants to meet you. My mama wants you to come to Sunday dinner next week."

Brielle turned toward him, surprised but smiling. "You want me to meet your family?"

"I want you there," he added honestly. "But only if you're comfortable."

She didn't hesitate long. "I'll go to Sunday dinner. As long as you come with me to my mama's on the Fourth."

"Cool, sounds like a deal," he told her.

As the next episode started playing, Taj leaned back into the couch, heart full, already imagining Brielle beside him at his mother's table. He would no longer be the lonely sibling because now he finally had someone to share life with.

THE SUN WAS high and bright when Taj pulled up in front of Denise's house, the quiet block transformed by the sound of music, laughter, and the smell of food cooking on the grill. Taj cut the engine and sat for a brief second, taking it all in. Taj had been around Brielle's family a few times, but never on the holiday and never as her man. As soon as he stepped out of the truck, he spotted Brielle through the open gate, already in the backyard. She stood near the patio, laughing with someone just out of view, the sunlight catching her skin and making her glow.

Taj walked through the wooden fence and stepped into the backyard, the smell of barbecue wrapping around him instantly. The backyard was decorated to perfection with string lights that hung from the corners of the fence even though it was still daylight, red and white checkered tablecloths covered folding tables, and small American flags were tucked into flowerpots and centerpiece jars. A cooler sat near the patio overflowing with ice and drinks, while a Bluetooth speaker played old-school R&B mixed with summer anthems. Brielle turned to him with a smile.

"You made it," she greeted, already moving toward him.

Taj didn't answer with words. He leaned down and kissed her. "You know I'm always going to show up for you. Happy Fourth, baby."

She smiled. "Happy Fourth."

His eyes scanned the yard briefly before returning to her. "Where's Nisaiah?"

"Inside with Amya," Brielle answered. "She snatched him the second she got here."

Taj chuckled and nodded, already turning toward the back door. "I figured."

Inside, the house was cooler and quieter, the noise of the backyard muffled the moment he stepped in. The living room was dimmer, curtains partially drawn to keep the heat out. Amya sat on the couch with Nisaiah cradled in her arms, his little body relaxed against her chest. She was talking softly to him, rocking him, as she watched TV. Taj stopped, smiling when he saw them.

"There go my little man," Taj spoke quietly.

Amya looked up and grinned. "Hey, Taj. He just ate and knocked right back out. Don't start nothing."

Taj didn't hesitate. He carefully scooped Nisaiah into his arms. The baby stirred, blinking up at him, before settling again, and Taj smiled down at him like nothing else in the world mattered. "Hey, little man," Taj murmured softly. "You enjoying your first Fourth?"

Nisaiah answered with a quiet grunt and a stretch, his tiny fingers curling into Taj's shirt. Taj adjusted his hold, rocking him gently, as he took his seat on the couch. He stayed inside with Nisaiah for about twenty minutes before finally putting him into his bassinet and walking back outside just to see more guests had arrived. Brielle called Taj over the moment she saw him walk out the house.

"I want you to meet some of my cousins," she spoke when he walked up. "This is Deja, Mike Mike, Peanut, and Shay. Y'all, this is Taj, my boyfriend."

Taj smiled, greeting each of them, and they greeted him. Taj enjoyed meeting more of Brielle's family. However, he enjoyed hearing her call him her boyfriend even more. Amya walked outside with Nisaiah in her arms, Brielle reaching for him the moment she walked up. The music got louder, plates filled up, and the smell of barbecue thickened the air. Taj was enjoying the vibe and enjoying the role of being Brielle's man even more.

Denise stepped out the back door with a huge smile on her face. Her hand was laced with a man's, and Taj watched as both Brielle and Amya stared at them. The man beside Denise was tall, a little over six feet, with brown skin and a salt-and-pepper beard that was trimmed neatly along his jaw. His hair was cut low, the gray at his temples. He wore dark jeans, a crisp white polo, and clean loafers. Denise guided him toward where Taj, Brielle, and Amya were standing.

"Everybody," Denise cooed, "this is my new boyfriend, Marcus."

Amya's mouth fell open. "Boyfriend?" she repeated, loud and dramatic. "Hold on. *Boyfriend,* as in ya man? As in you got a whole boo and didn't tell nobody?"

Denise shot her a look. "Girl, calm down."

Amya shook her head, eyes wide, as she looked Marcus up and down. "Nah, Mama D. I'm not even mad. I'm just shocked. You been holding out on us."

Marcus laughed easily, stepping forward and extending his hand. "Nice to meet you too," he greeted, clearly amused.

Brielle smiled, stepping in before Amya could say anything else reckless. "It's really nice to meet you," Brielle said sincerely. "I'm glad you came."

Marcus smiled back, warm and respectful. "I've heard a lot about you, Brielle."

They spent the rest of the day outside, the sun slowly giving way to dusk, as music poured from the speakers, and laughter filled every corner of the yard. Brielle danced barefoot on the grass with Amya, her hands in the air. Taj stayed close, sometimes swaying, as he held Nisaiah. He enjoyed laughing with her cousins and family friends over good food.

By the time fireworks started, Taj and Brielle had taken a seat on the grass. Denise had taken Nisaiah inside with her, and although there were still people in the yard, to Taj, it felt like it was only the two of them. Taj wrapped his arms around Brielle, and she leaned back against him, as they watched the light show.

"This is so beautiful," Brielle whispered, as she looked up into the sky.

"Yes, it is. But even more so because I'm watching them with you."

Brielle smiled, and they watched the fireworks until they were over. By the end, Taj was tired and ready to get home and wind down. He looked down at Brielle, who was still wrapped in his arms.

"It's late. I think it's about time I get outta here. You and Nisaiah coming home with me?"

Brielle nodded, letting Taj know she was coming. Taj stood to his feet before helping Brielle to hers. They walked into the house hand in hand. Denise was in the living room watching TV with Nisaiah next to her in his bassinet. Brielle began gathering his things and making sure everything was in his diaper bag, while Taj picked him up and put him in his car seat. Brielle kissed her mother goodbye before telling her that she would pick her car up sometime the next day. Taj hugged her as well before they walked out the door.

Taj drove them back to his place with Nisaiah sleeping in the backseat. When they pulled into Taj's driveway, they got out the car, and Taj grabbed Nisaiah before they walked into the house. Taj walked him upstairs and took him out of his seat before placing him in the bassinet he'd bought for him. He wanted somewhere for Nisaiah to sleep when they spent the night, so he felt it was only right. He had also bought him clothes, diapers, and formula for his house so that Brielle wouldn't have to pack for him when they stayed there.

Walking over to the nightstand by his bed that he kept Nisaiah's things in, he grabbed a onesie and a pair of socks. Brielle walked into the room just as Taj began taking the baby bathtub from his closet.

"I can give him a bath. You don't have to do all that, Taj."

"It's cool. I wanna have some alone time with his mama. And

I found that he sleeps all night if he gets a bath and a bottle before bed.”

Brielle smiled and nodded. When Taj was done bathing Nisaiah, he fed him and put him to sleep before placing him back into his bassinet. Taj made his way to the bathroom to take a shower himself. Brielle had already gone to another bathroom in the house and had taken her shower. So, when he returned to his bedroom and she was already lying in bed, he crawled in bed next to her.

“You wanna watch the rest of *The Blacklist*?” Taj asked.

“Nah. Tonight I’m trying to watch that black dick... in my mouth.”

Taj burst out into laughter, but Brielle didn’t make a peep, as she inched down and became eye length with his manhood. She wrapped her hands around his thick rod and licked the head. Taj gasped, as she took him in, the wetness of her mouth pulling her into him.

“Damnnn, what I do to deserve this?”

“I just want to please my man.”

Taj moaned a little louder, grabbing her head, as she took him deeper into her mouth. She slurped and sucked, as she watched his toes curl. Just when she knew he was about to cum, she sat up and straddled him, easing down on his manhood, as she guided him inside her.

“Fuckkkk!” he cursed, arching off the bed, as she rode him slowly.

She was so tight and wet that Taj felt as though he was going to cum each time she moved. He grabbed her ass cheeks, gripping them in his hands, as he guided her movements. Brielle leaned in, kissing him passionately, but never breaking his rhythm.

“Shit, you ridin’ the fuck out that dick, baby. That pussy feel so good.”

“It’s only for you, Daddy,” she whispered into his ear.

That was all it took for Taj to lose it. He began pumping upward, as Brielle rode him. His toes curled, and moans escaped from his lips until he couldn’t take anymore. He erupted inside her with her name on his tongue. When it was over, Taj wrapped his arms around Brielle tightly before they both fell asleep.

THAT FOLLOWING SUNDAY, Taj pulled up to Brielle's house at four on the dot, just like he'd promised. He sat in his car for a brief moment, hands resting on the steering wheel, nerves and excitement twisting together in his chest. This wasn't just another dinner. This was *the* dinner. The one where Brielle would finally meet his family. He checked his reflection in the rearview mirror, smoothed his shirt, then got out of the car.

Brielle stepped out onto the porch a moment later, locking the door behind her. She looked beautiful in a floral dress. Her braids were pulled back neatly, and she looked like she was glowing. When she walked down the steps toward him, Taj couldn't help the smile that spread across his face.

"You looked beautiful," he complimented.

"Thank you. You look very handsome yourself. I can't lie. I'm a little nervous."

"Don't be. It's nothing to be nervous about. I promise you my family will love you. Where is Nisaiah?"

"He's at Amya's house. I'm already nervous. I can't have him here too."

Taj nodded and opened Brielle's door for her. He walked around to the driver's seat and pulled out the driveway. Brielle didn't speak much on the drive there, and Taj knew it was because she was nervous. Taj grabbed her hand gently, as he glanced over at her.

"Calm down, baby. I promise you have nothing to worry about. They are all excited to meet you."

Brielle nodded her head but still stayed quiet. When they pulled up to the house, Taj parked in the driveway and got out the car. They walked up to the door together and walked inside. The smell of food cooking instantly hit Taj's nose.

"Mama, we're here," Taj announced.

"I'm in the kitchen, baby," Rita called out.

Taj took Brielle's hand and guided her through the house. Rita's eyes lit up the moment she saw Brielle. Dropping the dish towel onto the counter, she rushed over to them.

"Taj, she is beautiful. How you doing, sweetheart?"

"Thank you, Miss..."

"You better not call me Miss anything," Rita interrupted. "You can call me Rita or Mama, but that miss shit is for old ladies."

Brielle laughed. "Okay, Rita. My apologies."

"Tati and Tessa nem not here yet?" Taj asked.

"Nope, not yet, but they will be. You know they not gonna miss you bringing a woman home." Rita chuckled. "Taj ain't brought a woman home to meet us since his senior year of high school. It's safe to say that my son really likes you."

Brielle smiled. "Good, because I really like him too. Do you need help with anything?"

"Absolutely not. You are a guest in my home. You won't be lifting a finger in here today. The food is almost ready, and once everyone gets here, we can eat."

Brielle nodded, and both her and Taj took a seat at the kitchen table.

"See, I told you that she would love you," Taj whispered.

Brielle smiled back. "Yeah, you did."

They sat there and talked for about ten minutes, while Rita and Brielle got to know each other a little better. Right before Rita was about to take the food to the dining room table, Brielle informed Taj that she had to use the bathroom. Nodding his head, he took her hand and led her upstairs to the bathroom.

Chapter Seventeen

Brielle stood at the bathroom sink, as she washed her hands. She looked at herself in the mirror and smiled. She thought she was going to be super nervous about today. However, the moment she met Rita, she knew things were going to be fine. When Brielle came back from the bathroom, she walked back into the kitchen. Taj stood near the counter, laughing, and beside him was a woman Brielle hadn't seen yet with a little girl perched on a stool swinging her legs.

"Brielle," Taj said when he noticed her, his face lighting up. "Come here. I want you to meet my sister." He gently guided her closer. "This is Tati, and this little lady is my niece, Maleah."

Tati smiled wide, stepping forward and pulling Brielle into a quick, warm hug like they'd known each other longer than two minutes. "I am so happy to finally meet you," she spoke sincerely. "I've been hearing your name way too much not to."

Brielle laughed softly, instantly put at ease. "It's really nice to meet you too."

Before she could say anything else, Maleah leaned forward, studying her with serious little eyes. "You really pretty," Maleah announced.

The comment caught Brielle off guard, and her smile softened. She crouched slightly to meet the little girl's gaze. "Thank you, baby. You're really pretty too."

Maleah grinned, clearly pleased with herself.

Standing there, surrounded by Taj's family, Brielle felt her feelings shift. The nerves faded and were replaced by warmth. Nothing felt awkward or forced. Instead, it felt natural, like this was where she was supposed to be. She watched as Tati glanced toward the front of the house then checked her phone.

"Tessa and Hendrix should be pulling up with the girls any minute," she said casually. "She said they were ten minutes away when I talked to her."

"Good, because I'm ready to eat," Taj announced.

"Me too, Uncle Taj. Mommy wouldn't even let me have a snack or nothing," Maleah whined.

Rita's voice floated in from the dining room. "Tati, come help me take this food in here before it gets cold."

Tati rolled her eyes playfully. "Yes, ma'am," she replied back then looked at Brielle with a grin. "Welcome to Sunday dinner. You might not have to help now because you're a guest, but by next Sunday, her ass gon' be putting you to work."

Brielle laughed softly. "That's cool with me. I don't mind."

"You say that now," Tati joked, grabbing a tray and walking out the kitchen.

Brielle and Taj walked into the dining room to see the table was already set. Beautiful white china, cloth napkins, and shining crystal glasses sat at every place setting, with two candles in the middle of the table. Brielle was just about to tell Rita how beautiful the setup was when two little girls ran in, eyes wide and faces lit up with pure excitement. They made a beeline straight for Taj, wrapping their arms around him without hesitation.

"Uncle Taj!" one of them shouted.

Taj laughed, bracing himself, as he bent down to hug them both. "Hey, y'all. Uncle Taj missed y'all so much." He straightened up and gestured toward Brielle. "Brielle, these are two more of my nieces, Ashanti and Samia."

Ashanti, the older of the two, tilted her head slightly, studying

Brielle with open curiosity, while Samia smiled shyly but still managed a small wave.

"It's nice to meet you both," Brielle greeted warmly, her smile genuine. Seeing how close they were to Taj made her heart soften.

Before Brielle could say another word, the front door opened again. This time, a woman walked in carrying a toddler on her hip. She looked tired but put together, her hair pulled back neatly in a ponytail. She wore a white cropped t-shirt and a pair of light washed, distressed jeans. The little girl in her arms rested her head on her shoulder, her curls bouncing slightly, as she shifted.

"That's my sister, Tessa," Taj said quietly to Brielle, leaning in just enough for her to hear. "And that's my youngest niece, Chloe."

Brielle stepped forward, smiling. "It's really nice to meet you," she spoke, greeting Tessa.

Tessa returned the smile easily, adjusting Chloe on her hip. "Nice to meet you too. I've heard a lot about you."

Chloe peeked at Brielle from where she was tucked against her mother, blinking sleepily, before resting her head again. Taj wrapped his arm around Brielle's shoulder, and Brielle leaned into him.

"I told you they would love you," he whispered.

Tati glanced toward the front door then back at Tessa. "Where Hendrix at? Because I'm ready to eat," she announced, rubbing her hands together dramatically.

Tessa laughed. "He ran to the store real quick. Y'all can go ahead and start. He'll make his plate when he gets here."

Rita appeared at the head of the table, wiping her hands on a kitchen towel. "Alright then," she said firmly but warmly. "Everybody find a seat."

Chairs scraped against the floor, as everyone moved around the long table, kids settling wherever there was space, adults filling in around them. Brielle took a seat beside Taj, smoothing her dress as she sat. She looked around the table and couldn't help but smile at Taj's family.

Once everyone was settled, Rita looked toward Taj. "Go on, baby. Say grace."

Brielle turned her attention to him, curious. Taj straightened slightly, resting his forearms on the table. The room gradually quieted, even the kids sensing the shift.

"God," Taj began, his voice calm and steady, "we thank you for bringing us all together today. Thank you for family, for health, for love, and for another day. We ask that You bless this food and the hands that prepared it and keep your hands over us as we go through this week. Amen."

"Amen," everyone echoed.

As the food began getting passed around and conversation picked right back up, Brielle glanced at Taj, a soft smile on her lips. She was happy that Taj had introduced her to his family. Taj rested his hand on Brielle's knee under the table, rubbing it gently. She felt at home with his family, like she'd always been there. So, she knew the next time she came, she would bring her son for them to meet.

"So, how did you guys meet?" Tessa asked before taking a bite of a chicken wing.

"It's the craziest story." Brielle chuckled. "I actually hit his Rover and totaled my car. I was rushed to the hospital, and Taj sat down in the waiting room for hours until I was discharged."

"You got into an accident and fell in love? Girl, so what I gotta run? A red light or a stop sign? Do I fall out the car or onto him? Maleah need a step daddy," Tati spoke, looking over to Brielle.

All the adults burst out into laughter with the exception of Tati, who was still looking at Brielle, waiting on an answer.

"What y'all in here crackin' up about? Y'all in here having fun without me?" Hendrix asked, walking into the dining room.

"Daddy!" Samia called out cheerfully, as if she hadn't just seen him. "This is Uncle Taj girlfriend," she announced proudly. "Her name is Brielle."

The room seemed to slow. As she looked up at the man Samia called Daddy, the one everyone here knew to be Hendrix, the smile that had been on her face since she'd walked into the home vanished. Her stomach dropped so fast it felt like the floor disappeared beneath her. Standing there, just inside the dining room, keys still in his hand, was Delano. Her mouth fell open, as shock froze her in place.

He stopped short when he saw her; his face drained of color. His eyes widened, locking onto hers with unmistakable recognition. Taj felt the sudden tension immediately. The way Brielle's body stiffened beside him. The way her hand trembled where it rested on the table. He looked from her to Hendrix, confusion creasing his brow.

"Brielle? You good, baby?" Taj asked quietly.

But she couldn't answer him. Instead, she pushed her chair back so abruptly it scraped loudly against the floor. "Delano?!" she yelled, her voice sharp, shaking with disbelief. "Fuck you doing here?"

The room went silent. Tessa stood up almost immediately, confusion flashing across her face. "Um, his name is not Delano," she spoke, glancing between them. "It's Hendrix. And he's my husband."

"Hendrix, huh?" Brielle repeated, a bitter laugh breaking free, as anger surged through her chest. "Oh, so you lying about that shit too?"

Gasps rippled around the table, and Brielle didn't give a damn. She liked Taj a lot and respected him fully. However, this was about her son. She'd dreamed about what she would say to Delano when she saw him. What she would do. He'd abandoned her son and tried to make her life hard for no reason at all. So, if this was the place she saw him, then this was where she would handle business. She'd buried his betrayal for long enough, and today was the day it resurfaced.

Hendrix didn't say a word, just stood there, looking at her. Taj jumped up from his seat and rushed to Brielle's side.

"Brielle, baby. Tell me what's wrong," Taj urged.

"And why did you call him Delano? How do you even know my husband?" Tessa asked.

Her husband. The words hit Brielle like a ton of bricks. He was her husband and the father of her children. Brielle had been played yet again. Everything had been a lie. Brielle shook her head at the fact she even loved a man that she didn't even know. Anger shot through her when she realized that Taj's nieces were her son's siblings, the same little girls she'd helped him Christmas shop for and couldn't wait to meet.

"Sweetheart, you gonna have to start answering questions. I don't like all this drama in my house like this," Rita spoke firmly, looking over at Brielle.

"Bri, baby. Just talk to me. What's going on?" Taj spoke softly.

Finally, Brielle looked to Taj. "This sorry ass bitch that y'all know as Hendrix is Nisaiah's father!"

Tati gasped, covering her mouth, as she stood from the table. "Ashanti, take your sisters and cousin and y'all go upstairs and watch TV," Tati ordered, in a rush to get the children out the room.

"But I'm not done eating, Mommy," Maleah whined.

"Then take your plates but get upstairs now!" Rita ordered.

"We can eat upstairs, Grandma?" Samia asked, confused.

"Yes, now go!" Rita yelled, a little louder than she meant to.

The children took their plates with Ashanti taking Chloe's hand, and they all walked out the room. Tessa stepped closer, but Brielle never backed down, holding her gaze on Delano.

"This has to be some mistake. Who is Nisaiah?"

"Oh, no, ma'am. This is no mistake. This muthafucka is a liar, and he been lying to you and me. Nisaiah is my son, and this is the man that helped me create him. The same man that tried to hand me five thousand dollars to abort my baby because he said he didn't want kids. Yet he walks up in this muthafucka with three of them!"

"Hendrix, you better say something. Tell her this is a mistake," Tessa spoke.

Hendrix looked from Brielle to Tessa then back to Brielle again. "I have no clue who this woman is. This bitch lying. I ain't never seen her a day in my life, and I damn sure ain't got no fucking baby by her."

Slap!

With those words, Brielle reached up and slapped Hendrix dead across his face. "Oh, I'm a lying bitch? So, you saying we wasn't in a relationship for an entire year up until the moment I told you I was pregnant. You lying ass muthafucka!"

Hendrix stepped toward Brielle, as if he was going to hit her back, but Taj stepped between them. "I know Brielle, and one thing she's not is a liar. If she say that he's Nisaiah's father, then that's exactly what it is. And come to think about it, that little boy does look a lot like this nigga, sis," Taj said, looking over at Tessa. "And I would know seeing that I'm with him dam near every day."

"I know you not gonna believe this bitch over me, Taj. I thought we was family, bro."

"Watch yo' fuckin' mouth when you talkin' about my woman. I believe her because she ain't never gave me a reason not to. With that being said, that means you done hurt two women I love, which ain't gone end good for you."

"I'm telling y'all she lying!" Hendrix shot back.

"Oh, I'm lying? You don't fuckin' know me, huh?"

Brielle grabbed her purse and retrieved her phone. Putting in her password, she opened her photos and scrolled until she found some with her and Delano and handed her phone to Tessa.

"Does them pictures look like I'm lying to you?"

Tessa scrolled through the pictures with Tati behind her, looking at the phone over her shoulder. Tati gasped each time Tessa scrolled to a different picture.

"Now, Hendrix, you know you need yo' fucking ass beat. You over here lying with a straight ass face. You for sure know her," Tati spoke.

Tessa must have had enough before she dropped the phone on the table, balled a fist, and punched Hendrix dead in his face. "You fuckin' liar! You been cheating on me, and you had a fuckin' baby?"

Smack!

Tessa hit him again, this time open handed. The hit was so hard that it sent Hendrix stumbling backwards. Tears fell from Tessa's face, while Tati and Rita stood there with their hands covering their mouths. Taj stood next to Brielle, guarding her, his eyes locked on Hendrix.

"Baby, look, okay, I fucked up. I fucked her, okay? I was stupid and had a moment of weakness. But I don't know shit about no kid. I have three little girls, and that's it," Hendrix confessed, as he tried to walk closer to Tessa.

"You have a fucking four month old son too. But of course you wouldn't know anything about him because you ain't been around since the day I told you I was pregnant," Brielle chimed in.

"Four months!?" Rita yelled out. "Hendrix."

"Bitch, I'm fuckin' sick of you. You wanna come in here and ruin my life just because yo' shit fucked up? I told you to get rid of that baby. I told you I didn't want to have no fuckin' kids by you, not that I didn't want kids. I have three already and a wife. They are who I want. But you so miserable that you want to ruin that shit. Bitch, I should beat yo' fuckin' ass."

Hendrix charged toward Brielle, but before he could make contact, Taj jumped on him, punching him twice in the face, before Hendrix fell to the floor. Taj didn't stop punching and kicking him bloody. He didn't stop until he finally heard his mother's voice telling him to. When Taj finally stood to his feet, Hendrix was balled up on the floor, a bloody mess.

Slowly, Hendrix sat up, using the chair to help him stand to his feet. He stumbled toward Tessa. "Please, baby, can we just talk about this?"

"It ain't shit to talk about. Get the fuck out of my mama's house. Now!"

Hendrix nodded his head slowly before leaving the dining room and walking out the house. Brielle stood there, looking around the room at the chaos she'd started. Tessa was crying, Taj was angry, and Rita and Tati just looked like they didn't know what to do. The Sunday dinner she had been so excited about had turned into one big mess. Embarrassed, Brielle grabbed her purse and the phone from the table.

"I'm so sorry about everything. I should leave," she announced before rushing out the house.

Chapter Eighteen

Brielle stood outside, scrolling through her phone, as she tried to locate the Uber app. Tears streamed down her face, as she stood there, wishing she'd drove her own car. Her phone was clenched in one hand and her purse in the other. She was seething. Delano, who she found out wasn't Delano but Hendrix, was married with three children.

The lies replayed in her head like a broken record. The fake loft, the money he'd tried to give her to abort their son, it all hit her at once – the way he'd looked her in the eye and told her that he loved her, all the while having a wife at home. Brielle's heart seemed to be breaking all over again, this time not only for her but for her son as well. And beneath all the rage was deep, sinking embarrassment. She'd completely shown her ass in front of Taj's family. She'd allowed months of pain to spill out in front of total strangers. And worst of all, in front of Taj.

That man had done nothing but show up for her and her son, every time. He'd loved her quietly and patiently, without asking for anything in return. *Damn, the one thing he wanted me to do for him, I couldn't even do without having bullshit follow me. All he wanted me to do was meet his family, and I couldn't even do that shit for him,* Brielle thought, and her chest tightened. She heard the door open behind her but didn't turn around. She didn't have to because she felt him.

"Brielle," Taj said softly.

Just hearing her name on his lips made her eyes burn.

She shook her head immediately. "I-I can't. I just need to go," she spoke, her voice cracking.

Taj stepped closer. "Please, baby, you don't have to go."

"Yes, I do. You were in there just like I was. You saw what happened. Then I put you right in the middle of it. That's your brother-in-law, your sister's husband, and you fought him, Taj. That shit went down in front of your mother. And I'm sure your sister hates me. She came to Sunday dinner and got her entire life ruined, and it's all because of me."

"No! It's because of him," he said firmly. "You told the truth. That nigga was the only one lying." Taj reached for her, looking Brielle directly in the eye. "Please don't leave, baby."

The Uber pulled up to the curb, and Brielle turned away from Taj, walking toward the car. "I'm sorry," she whispered, finally turning toward him. Her eyes were glossy, and her face was tight with emotion. She got into the car before he could even say a word, tears sliding down her face the moment she pulled away.

She'd ordered the Uber to take her to Amya's house, knowing she needed to talk to her best friend and hold her son. She called Amya the moment they pulled onto her street, telling her to open the door. Amya must have known something was wrong because she had the door open before Brielle could even walk up the steps. She stood there in pajamas and a bonnet, Nisaiah already in her arms, as she waited for Brielle to walk through the door.

The second Brielle stepped inside the house, she broke, tears streaming from her eyes. Her purse slid off her shoulder and hit the floor, as she crumpled forward, landing next to it, hands flying to her face. A sound tore out of her that didn't even feel human.

"Oh, my God, Bri, what's wrong?" Amya asked instantly, shifting Nisaiah to one arm and wrapping the other around Brielle. "Come here."

Brielle collapsed into her best friend's chest, sobbing so hard her knees buckled. Amya helped her up and guided her to the couch, sitting her down and pulling her into an embrace.

"What's wrong, bestie? Did Taj do something?"

Brielle shook her head. "No, it's me. I let this happen."

"You let what happen?"

"I saw Delano for the first time today since he left, and I showed my natural black ass," Brielle announced, taking Nisaiah from Amya and cradling him in her arms.

"What do you mean you saw Delano? I thought you said you were going to Sunday dinner at Taj's mama's house. Where did you see him?"

"Well, apparently, Delano's real name is Hendrix, and he's married to Taj's sister, and they have three kids."

"Wwhaattt? Are you serious?"

"It was so bad. Shit got physical."

"Oh, my God, you hit him?" Amya asked.

"I was just so mad. It was like all the hurt came rushing back to me the moment I saw his face. But then I showed Taj's sister, Tessa, all the pictures of us in my phone when Delano tried to say he didn't know me, and she popped his ass upside the head a few times. But the real fight is when Taj stepped in. Taj beat the hell out of him in front of his entire family, and I just feel so bad. I really like Taj, but I know I can never be with him again."

Amya shifted her body so that she could be eye to eye with Brielle. "Okay, one thing at a time. What do you mean you can never see Taj again? Why would that stop your relationship?"

"What? Girl, I slept with his sister's husband. We have a child together. Taj's nieces are my son's siblings. Are you not seeing how messy this shit is?"

Amya nodded her head in understanding. "Yes, it's very messy, I'll give you that. But this shit ain't yo' fault. How the hell was you supposed to know that Delano was a married father of three named Hendrix?"

"I just feel so stupid. I lost it in front of everyone – the kids, his mom. And I know his sister has to hate me. Now, I'll forever be known as the girlfriend that brought all the drama to Sunday dinner. I just feel so stupid."

"First of all," Amya spoke firmly, "you are not stupid. You were blindsided," Her eyes never left Brielle's.

Brielle shook her head. "I embarrassed Taj. I embarrassed myself. I didn't want him to see me like that."

Amya let out a sharp breath. "Nah. What you not finna do is put this on you. Did Taj tell you that you embarrassed him? Did he tell you that he didn't want to see you anymore?"

"No, he actually wanted me to stay. He asked me not to leave, but I was so embarrassed there was no way I could walk back into that house. I know his family has to hate me."

"Well, it's a good thing you not the family's girlfriend. You're his. Let him handle his family and you handle your relationship. That man don't want to lose you and even I know that. Don't allow Delano to take your happiness. You deserve this."

"This shit is just too complicated, Mya. Did you hear me say my son and his sister's children are siblings? How can this work?"

"Girl, just like it's been workin'. Brielle, Taj loves you, like really loves you, and has since the day he met you. I don't think none of that shit even matters to him, honestly. I mean, you said yourself that he asked you not to leave."

Amya got up from the couch and walked into her kitchen, returning a few moments later with a bottle of wine and two glasses. Brielle stood up and placed a sleeping Nisaiah into his playpen before sitting back on the couch. Amya opened the bottle and poured the two glasses before taking a sip from one. They sat on the couch for hours, just talking. Once the bottle of wine was finished and they were both a little tipsy, Brielle decided to spend the night at Amya's house and just go home in the morning.

She walked upstairs, cradling Nisaiah in her arms, and went into the guest bedroom. Amya brought her a pair of shorts and a shirt to sleep in, and after Brielle changed her clothes, she laid down in bed, cuddling Nisaiah's small body in her arms. Tears rolled from her eyes, as the weight of the day settled deep in her chest. Finally, after hours of just staring at the wall, Brielle was able to drift off to sleep.

———

AMYA PULLED into Brielle's driveway just after nine the next morning. The sun was already high, casting soft light across the quiet street, but Brielle's stomach tightened the moment she noticed the familiar black Range Rover parked in her driveway.

Amya saw him too and smiled instantly. "Mmm," she said knowingly, as she put the car in park. "Look who's right here waiting on you."

Brielle didn't respond right away. Her emotions tangled all over again. Guilt from the night before and nerves came rushing in. She unbuckled herself and getting out the car before grabbing Nisaiah, lifting him out of his car seat and settling him against her chest.

"You can keep this car seat for your car, I have another one," Brielle voiced before closing the door.

The driver's door of Taj's truck opened just as she stepped out of Amya's car. Taj stepped out, exhaustion all over his face. He was still in the same clothes he had on at dinner, and his eyes were slightly red, like he hadn't slept. However, the moment he saw Brielle and Nisaiah, his entire expression changed.

"Morning," he greeted quietly, as he walked toward her.

"Hey," Brielle replied, her voice just as soft.

She shifted Nisaiah higher on her shoulder. "You... you been sitting out here all night?"

Taj nodded without hesitation. "Yeah."

Her brows pulled together. "Taj... you..."

"I wasn't leaving until I knew you was okay," he interrupted.

Emotion pressed against her chest, thick and sudden. She glanced down at her son then back up at Taj. "You didn't have to do that."

"Yes, I did," he replied.

Amya cleared her throat lightly, as she poked her head out the window slightly. "I'm gonna head out." She grinned. "Call me later."

Brielle nodded, watching as Amya drove off, leaving the three of them standing there in her driveway. Brielle took a deep breath then gestured toward the house.

"You wanna come inside?"

Taj nodded. "Yeah."

They walked up the driveway together, Taj opening the door for her like it was second nature. Brielle stepped inside with Nisaiah in her arms, Taj following closely behind. He took a seat on the couch, while Brielle carried Nisaiah down the short hallway, her movements slow and careful. He stirred when she lowered him into his crib, his little fingers curling against the blanket, but he didn't wake. Brielle kissed his forehead gently, watching him for a second longer.

When she finally turned to walk out the room, Taj was leaning against the doorframe, watching her quietly. They walked back into the living room without speaking. The silence wasn't awkward, just thick with everything they hadn't said yet. As soon as she stopped moving, Taj stepped into her space and pulled her into his arms. The hug wasn't gentle at first. It was tight, almost desperate, like he needed to feel her against him. Brielle's breath caught, as her cheek pressed into his chest, the familiar scent of him wrapping around her. Her hands hesitated for half a second before gripping the back of his shirt, fingers curling into the fabric like she was afraid he might disappear if she let go.

"Taj..." she whispered, but her voice broke before she could finish.

He pulled back just enough to look at her, his hands framing her face. His thumbs brushed under her eyes, slow and reverent, like he was memorizing her. He leaned down and kissed her deeply. Brielle melted into it, the tension she'd been carrying since the night before finally cracking. Her lips moved with his instinctively, emotion flooding her so fast it made her dizzy. When they parted, their foreheads stayed pressed together.

"I love you," Taj spoke firmly, like he needed her to hear it exactly as it was meant. "And I don't want you going anywhere."

Her throat tightened instantly, the words echoing in her chest, heavy and beautiful yet terrifying all at once.

"Taj..." she breathed, her eyes stinging. "This whole situation..."

"Stop," he spoke, shaking his head. "None of this is your fault. None of it."

She swallowed, emotion clawing its way up. "It feels like it is," she admitted. "Like everything blew up because of me. Because I couldn't keep my emotions in check. I just wish things would have went down differently."

He leaned down slightly, so they were eye to eye. "I'm glad things went down the way they did. If not, my sister would still be living a lie. My nieces have a sibling they didn't even know about. You didn't break anything, Brielle. You exposed what was already broken."

Her eyes dropped, tears finally spilling over. "I just keep thinking about how this is supposed to work?" she asked, her voice trembling. "Your family has to hate me after this."

Taj exhaled slowly then lifted her chin, so she had to look at him. "They don't hate you."

She gave a small, disbelieving shake of her head. "Taj..."

"They don't," he repeated more firmly. "If anything, they respect you."

"Respect me... for what?"

"For being brave enough to tell the truth. You could have said nothing and allowed my sister to live in a loveless marriage. You didn't come in trying to tear my family apart. You walked in as a woman ready to meet her man's family. Instead, you were blindsided by the ghosts of your past. Baby, he did this, not you."

Brielle's breath shook, as she let his words sink in. Part of her wanted to believe him so badly it hurt. Another part was still guarded, still bracing for the disappointment of reality. This wasn't the ideal situation at all, and she didn't want to get more attached to Taj just to have it all come crashing down.

"I don't want to keep putting Nisaiah in the middle of chaos."

Taj pulled her back into his chest, this time holding her closer. His hand rubbed slow circles over her back. "I don't want that either. And I would never put him or you in that situation. If I even thought it would be drama, I would tell you. You have to know that. I want the best for you and Nisaiah."

Brielle looked into Taj's eyes, everything in her wanting to believe him. Taj had shown up every single time for her, proving that he had her back. However, it wasn't just her that she had to think about. What would her son think when he got older, and he had sisters that called Taj uncle? She didn't know if they were supposed to grow up as siblings or cousins. What would she do if and when Hendrix came back around? It was all just too much for her.

"Taj, I just don't know if I can. This is a lot, and it's so much to figure out. I'm not saying I want to break up, but I need time to think about how this could even work and what we do from here."

"We take it one day at a time together. I love you, Brielle. I've known that since the day you hit my Rover, and the only thing I was concerned about was you. You need time; that's fine. But when you're ready, I'll be right here. All I want is you, and I'm not going anywhere."

Taj reached into his back pocket and pulled out a folded envelope and handed it to her. Brielle looked down, confused, as she took it from him.

"I meant what I said. I only want what's best for you. If time is what's best, then take all the time you need."

Taj kissed Brielle on the forehead before walking out the door. Brielle wanted to stop him, tell him to stay and hold her, but instead, she stood there and said nothing. She sat on the couch, slowly opening the envelope, and pulled out several pieces of folded paper. She read the first page and saw it was the deed to her house with her name on it as the owner. Her mouth dropped open, as she read every word to make sure it was correct. *Oh, my*

God, he bought this house for me, she thought, as tears streamed down her face.

She flipped through to the next paper. It was an account with her name on it and ten thousand dollars in it. She did a double take at the account, knowing that she hadn't started it. The next piece of paper was a note from Taj.

> *Hey, Bri,*
>
> *I didn't know when the right time would be to give you this, but I figured with everything going on that now was the time. You have never rented this house. The house has belonged to you since the day you moved in. I wanted to give you the gift of stability, and this is my way of doing so. The other paper is a bank account that I started. I put the rent you paid to Rick in it and matched it each month. No matter what happens between us, I will continue to match what you deposit. You can save the money for a rainy day or for a college fund for Nisaiah. The choice is yours. I love you, Brielle, and I just want you to know that.*
>
> *Taj*

Tears streamed from Brielle's eyes, as she held the papers close to her heart. If this wasn't a way to show someone that you loved them, Brielle didn't know what was. After seeing this, there was no way she could let Taj go. *That's a good man, my good man, and I'm gonna stick beside him.*

Chapter Nineteen

"Wait a minute, bitch. That nigga bought a house for you and put money in the bank for Nisaiah, and you just let him leave?" Amya yelled into the phone.

"I didn't open the envelope until he was already gone."

"Then why the fuck are you on the phone with me and not him? Bitch, hang up and call that man now."

"But I told him I needed space," Brielle replied.

"And you took the space that you needed to read the letter he left you. I'm hanging up. Call that man now."

Before Brielle could say anything, Amya ended the call. Brielle couldn't do anything but laugh, knowing her best friend was right. She sat there, on her couch, with her phone clutched in her hand. She hesitated for just a moment before finally calling Taj. He answered on the first ring, his voice deep and steady.

"Please come back," she spoke.

"I'm already on my way."

Brielle smiled, stood up, and opened the door for him. Not even five minutes later, he was walking through it. He rushed over to Brielle, grabbing her up and pulling her into a kiss.

"Don't play with me because I don't play about you. I don't want to be without you," Taj spoke between kisses.

"I don't want to be without you either."

With those words, Taj took her hand and led her to the bedroom. She was already wet when she laid on the bed, in anticipation of what was about to take place. Taj pulled off the sweat pants she'd taken from Amya's dresser that morning, tossing them to the floor. Getting on his knees, he grabbed her thighs and pulled her toward him.

"You can't take this away from me," he whispered before placing gentle kisses on her love box.

Brielle gasped, as he moved his tongue in slow circles. She tossed her leg over his shoulder, arching off the bed slightly, as she gripped his head. Her body trembled, as he brought her to an orgasm instantly, causing her to fall back onto the bed, her breaths uneven. Taj wasted no time standing to his feet and removing his clothes. Brielle smiled, as she saw his thick manhood standing at attention. Sitting up, she moved to the edge of the bed. She leaned forward, wrapping her hands around his manhood, but just before she went to put it in her mouth, he stopped her.

"This is about you. Lay back down," Taj ordered.

Brielle did as she was told, laying back onto the bed with her legs spread wide. Taj nestled himself between her thighs, inserting his thickness inside her slowly. She yelped, wrapping her arms around him and holding him tightly. Taj moaned into her neck, as he inched deeper into her wetness. She wrapped her legs around him, holding him deep inside her, as she moved her hips in slow circles. She wanted to make him feel just as good as he was making her feel.

"You feel so good," Brielle whispered, still holding Taj close to her.

Brielle closed her eyes, letting herself feel everything he was giving her. Their bodies moved together, syncing with the same rhythm, their moans being the music they moved to. Brielle felt every stroke, and she opened wider so that he could go even deeper. They climaxed at the same time, moaning loudly as they finished.

Taj rolled over, holding her close. Lacing their fingers together, they laid there for a moment, just wrapped in each other. Brielle exhaled and closed her eyes. For once in her life, she felt truly loved, and as she laid there cradled in his arms, she finally said it.

"I love you too, Taj."

THE LATE-AFTERNOON SUN sat high and warm in the sky, as Taj turned onto his mother's street. Brielle sat in the passenger seat with Nisaiah strapped securely into his car seat behind her, her hand resting on her lap simply. Her stomach fluttered the moment they pulled into Rita's driveway. She hadn't been back to Taj's mother's house since everything had blown up, and even now, weeks later, the memory still made her chest tighten. She inhaled slowly, reminding herself that this was different. Everything was out in the open, and Taj had assured her that she didn't have anything to worry about.

She glanced back at Nisaiah. He was awake, his big eyes curious, as he took in the light and movement outside the window, one tiny fist tucked beneath his chin. Taj reached over and squeezed her knee gently. She looked at him and caught the small, reassuring smile on his face.

"You okay?" he asked softly.

She nodded, though her emotions were layered. She wanted today to be good – not just for her sake but for Taj as well. She wanted to believe that what he'd told her was true, that his family didn't see her as a problem but as a woman who had simply told the truth when it mattered. Her heart beat faster, as Taj turned the engine off. This wasn't just a Sunday dinner. It was a reopening of a door she hadn't been sure would unlock again. She straightened her dress, suddenly aware of everything.

Taj got out the car first, walking around to the back to unbuckle Nisaiah, taking him from his car seat. Brielle watched him with a smile. No matter what had happened, Taj still treated her son like he was his, and that was all Brielle could ask for. She opened her door and stepped out into the summer heat. The moment her feet touched the driveway, reality settled in fully. This was it, and there was no turning back now. She took a steadying breath, as Taj came to her side and handed Nisaiah to her, as they walked up the driveway.

The moment they stepped inside, the cool air of the house wrapped around Brielle, carrying the familiar scent of lemon cleaner. Rita stood at the front door as if she'd seen them pull up and was waiting for them to walk in.

"There you are," Rita uttered warmly, pulling Brielle into a hug that was firm and genuine. "I'm so glad you came, baby."

The words loosened a knot that had been sitting tight in her chest. She hugged her back, a little hesitant at first, then more fully when she felt how sincere the embrace was. Rita's attention shifted immediately to Nisaiah, her eyes softening, as she reached out.

"And look at him," she cooed, smiling wide. "My goodness, he's so cute."

Brielle smiled, pride warming her voice. "Thank you."

"Can I hold him?" Rita asked, already extending her arms.

"Of course," Brielle replied, carefully handing Nisaiah to her.

Rita cradled him, rocking him gently, as she sat down on the couch. She murmured to him softly, admiring his chunky cheeks and wide eyes. Brielle sat beside her, watching with a mix of relief and emotion. Seeing Rita with her son made her fears settle. Taj dropped into the chair across from them, his gaze moving between Brielle and Nisaiah, a quiet smile resting on his face. A few minutes later, the front door opened again, and familiar voices filled the room.

"Brielle!" Maleah called out, as she came in with Tati close behind her.

Tati's face broke into a grin when she saw Brielle. "Girlll, I thought you was never coming back. I been asking Taj about you. I'm glad you're here."

The words meant more than Brielle could easily explain. "Me too," she replied.

"Is this your baby, Brielle?" Maleah asked, already rushing over to Rita.

"Yes, this is Nisaiah," Brielle replied. "Would you like to hold him?

Maleah smiled, wide eyed, as she nodded her head up and down. Brielle told her to sit back on the couch, and Maleah did so quickly. Brielle smiled, taking Nisaiah from Rita and placing him on Maleah's lap. She watched as Maleah talked to Nisaiah.

"You so good with him, Lele. Tell yo' mama to give you a little brother or sister to play with," Rita joked.

"Oh, no, ma'am. I'm not having any more kids until I get married. And even then, it's in the air." Tati laughed.

Rita laughed before nodding her head. "I hear you, but you know I want all the grandkids I can get." Rita laughed before looking at the clock on the wall. "We're just waiting on Tessa and the girls now. They should be here any minute, then we all can eat."

Brielle nodded, settling back into the couch. A few moments later, Nisaiah began to fuss in Maleah's arms. She knew that he was probably hungry and needed to be changed, so she stood to her feet, taking him into her arms and grabbing the diaper bag. Taj told her she could change him in his old room before he led her up the stairs and down the hall. The room was small and full of Michigan State memorabilia.

"Just come back down when you're done," Taj spoke before walking back downstairs.

She laid Nisaiah on the twin sized bed before changing his diaper. When she was done, she made him a bottle and fed him before making her way back downstairs. She froze when she saw Tessa standing in the middle of the living room, all three of her girls right next to her. However, who Brielle didn't see was Hendrix, and that put her at ease even more.

"Hey, Brielle, can I talk to you for a minute?" Tessa asked the moment Brielle walked down the stairs.

"Sure," she replied.

Tessa nodded and motioned for Brielle to follow her through

the house. The sliding glass door came into view, sunlight spilling through it, warm and golden, casting long shadows across the floor. Nisaiah shifted in her arms, letting out a small, restless sound that immediately pulled Brielle's attention back to him. She adjusted her grip instinctively, resting his head more securely against her chest. Being here already had her nerves tight, and now Tessa wanted to talk privately, which made Brielle even more nervous.

When the door slid open, the backyard greeted them with the sounds of summer. The air smelled like freshly cut grass and charcoal from someone close by grilling. The backyard looked peaceful, with the patio furniture neatly arranged and sunlight filtering through the trees that lined the fence. It wasn't until they stepped fully outside that Brielle really looked down at her arms and realized she was still holding Nisaiah. Her chest tightened. *Shit!* The thought hit her all at once. *This is her husband's baby. I didn't even consider how she would feel seeing him.* The reality of it pressed against her ribs, as she realized the pain this had to be causing. No matter how much time had passed, no matter how much truth had come out, that part of the situation didn't change. She imagined what it must feel like for Tessa to see this child, living proof of her husband's betrayal, cradled so easily in her arms.

"Shit, let me take him inside," Brielle said quickly, already turning back toward the house. Her voice came out softer than she expected, layered with unease. "I don't..." She didn't finish the sentence, but the rest of it lived in her eyes.

She took a step toward the door, her movements careful, protective. Her instinct was to shield Nisaiah from anything tense or heavy, even emotions he couldn't yet understand. The idea of standing in front of Tessa with him in her arms suddenly felt wrong, like crossing a line she hadn't meant to step over. Before she could reach the door, Tessa's hand gently closed around her wrist.

"Brielle," Tessa said, her voice calm but firm, "you don't have to take him inside. He can stay out here with us."

Brielle stopped mid-step, her body stiffening slightly, as she turned back to face her. Tessa gave her a half smile, and Brielle nodded her head. They both took their seats on the bench, Tessa turning to face Brielle.

"I want you to know that I don't blame you for any of this. No matter what you think, it's nothing that anybody can tell me about that man that I didn't already know. So, the moment you said that he was your son's father, I knew it was true."

"I'm so sorry, Tessa. Never in a million years did I think this would happen. I didn't even know he was married until that day."

"And that's his fault, not yours. We both fell victim to the same nigga's bullshit."

"Ain't that the truth," Brielle replied.

"I ain't never told nobody this; hell, I don't even know why I'm saying it now. But the truth is I knew I needed to leave him about two years into our marriage. I honestly don't know what made me stay so long. This not the first time he's cheated. This is just the first time he got caught and couldn't lie his way up out of it. It's almost like I been looking for a reason to leave. Two weeks before you came to Sunday dinner, I asked God to reveal who my husband really was and if he was not supposed to be in my life to remove him. Now look at God."

"I still feel so bad. The entire situation is just messy, especially from the outside looking in," Brielle replied.

"Girl, fuck outsiders. Their opinions don't matter. We know what happened and how it went down. And hell, they shit messy too. They just can't own their shit the way we can. My brother loves you, so that means we're family now. We can figure the rest of that shit out as we go."

Brielle nodded her head. "So, he won't be coming around any time soon?"

"Not unless you bring him because he damn sure don't want to see me again. The way I beat the hell out of him when he came home that night, I'd be surprised if that nigga can see at all for the next few months." Tessa chuckled.

"Girllll, I know you didn't." Brielle laughed. "Not you beat his ass."

"Shiiitttt! You remember Regina King's character from *This Christmas*? Oh, okay."

"You had him sliding across the floor?"

"Girl, like a damn slip and slide."

Tessa and Brielle both laughed, the moment being something they both needed. There was no animosity or grudges being held, just two women that had been hurt by the same man healing together. They stayed outside, talking for a few more moments, before the sliding door opened, and Taj appeared.

"I'm just coming out here to make sure y'all good," Taj voiced, only half teasing.

"Everything is great. I'ma go inside and help Mama set the table. I know she was trying to act like she was waiting on me to get here, but I know it's something that gotta be done before we eat." Tessa smiled at Brielle once more before walking back into the house.

"Everything good for real, baby?" Taj asked again, this time walking closer to Brielle.

"Yeah, everything is great. Are you good?" she asked with a smile.

"I been good since the day you came colliding into me. But right now, I'm over the moon."

Brielle smiled, leaning up to kiss Taj, Nisaiah resting his head on her shoulder. It wasn't until that moment that Brielle felt completely safe. Everything she'd been through had led her to this moment with this man, and that was when her heart knew what true love felt like.

The End

Did You Enjoy?

Did you enjoy the read?
Let us know how much by leaving us a
review on Amazon and Goodreads.

Other Books By

URBAN AINT DEAD

Tales 4rm Da Dale

The Hottest Summer Ever

Hittin' Licks For The Holidays: Atlanta

Wet Dreams On Lockdown: The Nurse

How To Publish A Book From Prison

How To Invest In The Stock Market From Prison

First Summer Out With My Prison Bae

By **Elijah R. Freeman**

Despite The Odds

Despite The Odds 2

By **Juhnell Morgan**

Hittaz

Hittaz 2

Hittaz 3

Hittaz 4

Hittaz 5

Hittaz 6

Coldhearted

Coldhearted 2

Coldhearted 3

By **Lou Garden Price, Sr.**

A Hitman's Gift For Christmas

A YN'S Muse For The Summer

Wizdom: Forever Your Gangsta

Charge It To The Game

Charge It To The Game 2

Charge It To The Game 3

A Summer To Remember With My Hitta

Snatched Up By A Hitta

Santa Sent Me A Real One For Christmas

Wet Dreams On Lockdown: The Unit Manager

Thug Me The Right Way 2

Thug Me The Right Way 3

Seizing A Gangsta's Heart For The Summer

Yours For The Taking

Wrapped Up In A Hitta's Love For Christmas

By **Nai**

A Set Up For Revenge

A Set Up For Revenge 2

Wet Dreams On Lockdown: The Librarian

By **Ashley Williams**

Trickin' On A Heaux For Christmas

Homie Hoppin' For The Holidays

Wet Dreams On Lockdown: The Female C.O

Letters Of His Love

By **Telia Teanna**

The State's Witness

The State's Witness 2

The State's Witness 3

This Time Won't You Save Me

This Time Won't You Save Me 2

His Summer Side Piece

A Holiday Heist

Healing The Heart Of A Detroit Gangsta

Summer Vows With A Detroit Gangsta

The Promissory

The Promissory 2

A Gangsta's Last Kiss

What Do The Lonely Do At Christmas

By **Kyiris Ashley**

Stuck In The Trenches

Stuck In The Trenches 2

By **Huff Tha Great**

Melted The Heart Of A Menace

Wet Dreams On Lockdown: Lieutenant Grace

By **P. Wise**

Merry Trapmas

By **Mia Sky**

Thug Me The Right Way

By **DiamondATL & Nai**

Wet Dreams On Lockdown: The Counselor

By **Paris Iman**

Wet Dreams On Lockdown: The Male C.O

By **Tamyra Griffin**

Wet Dreams On Lockdown: The Captain

By **TN Jones**

Wet Dreams On Lockdown: The Warden

By **Shawnice**

Atlantastan

Atlantastan 2

Atlantastan 3

By **Chris Green**

IN The Streetz

IN The Streetz 2

IN The Streetz 3

IN The Streetz 4

IN The Streetz 5

IN The Streetz 6

Hittin' Licks For The Holidays: Charleston

By **Tron Hill**

Hittin' Licks For The Holidays: New York

Bandemic

Bandemic 2

By **Freshh Moneyy**

Coming Soon From
URBAN AINT DEAD

Drill
The Hottest Summer Ever 2
THE G-CODE
Tales 4rm Da Dale 2
How To Build Your Credit From Prison
By **Elijah R. Freeman**

Despite The Odds 3
By **Juhnell Morgan**

A Felon's Promise
By **Nai**

Kenzo Steele
By Kyiris Ashley

To Die For
By **Tron Hill**

Bandemic 3
By Freshh Moneyy